THE CHOSEN

Dawn Lee Daley

Printed by CreateSpace

An Amazon.com Company

Dawn Lee Daley
www.angelchroniclebooks.com

This is a work of fiction. Names, characters, places, and incidents are a product of the author's imagination. Locales and public names are sometimes used for atmospheric purposes. Any resemblance to actual people, living or dead, or to businesses, companies, events, institutions, or locales is completely coincidental.

Book Layout © 2017 BookDesignTemplates.com
Edited by: Erin Liles (www.inaperfectword.com)

Angel Chronicles: The Chosen/Dawn Lee Daley -- 1st ed.
ISBN 978-0692882276 (paperback)

To every broken soul—you are more than enough.

"For many are invited, but few are chosen."

—MATTHEW 22:14 NIV

17 YEARS AND 9 MONTHS AGO

Elizabeth's eyes gave way in a hesitant flutter. After a fitful night of sleep, she found herself sprawled out in the middle of a warm, radiant light, and even with bleary eyes, she could see that she was still in her own room. She felt lighter now that she was finally awake. She nuzzled into the warmth of her pillow pressed against her face, relished in the softness of her bed sheets as they skimmed over her legs, and came back to reality when she felt the resistance from her bed.

Surrounded by a supernatural brilliance and overwhelmed by the presence of total calm Elizabeth felt an unknown force tug at her heart, guiding her to rest her hand on her stomach right below her belly button. She took in a deep breath and closed her eyes again, letting this peace wash over her.

In this moment, where time stood still, she understood; her and Dean's prayers were at last answered. Years had gone by while they had prayed and waited for a child.

When she opened her eyes once more, an ethereal masculine figure stood before her. He was frighteningly tall, formidable, awe-inspiring. His skin was a dark bronze, bathed by golden light from head to toe. From his shoulders dawned resolute wings covered with the purest of white feathers. Each feather was tipped with gold and sparkled in the light. Elizabeth could not handle looking straight at him, the light was near blinding.

In a deep, resolute voice the figure before her began to speak.

"God has heard your prayers, Elizabeth. He has entrusted you with this precious, innocent soul. This child will have a great destiny, one that comes with much sacrifice. God has sent me here to bless her. To give her abilities that will equip her in her purpose so that even in her weaknesses she will find strength. Guide her well in the ways of the Lord, Elizabeth. Never forget that in all things, God is with you." As quickly as the angel arrived, he disappeared.

Elizabeth fell to her knees in awe and wonder, thanking God. She thanked Him for the blessing of this child. She shook from excitement and joy. She had waited so long for this moment. She was patiently ready to meet this blessing from God; and though she had no worldly proof, Elizabeth knew she carried a miracle.

CHAPTER 1

SELAH

Selah's head began to throb, the pressure gathering tighter around her temples. Sean, her brother, continued to fray her last nerve. Gritting her teeth, she growled, "Sean. Listen. Seriously, stop asking me!" Selah was in no mood for his games right now. If he asked her for a ride one more time, the seething frustration she was trying hard to hold back was going to detonate.

"Come on, Sis! Daniel and Tony will be there. Show your little brother some love, will ya?"

Selah rolled her eyes. "Did you even talk to Mom about it?" The last time she had given Sean a ride somewhere, he ended up at a different party altogether by sneaking off with his friends. Selah never told their mom about it because she did not want to stress her out. But the more she thought about it, she should've, because that would mean Sean would not be going out tonight.

"Yeah, she knows." He stood there, all nonchalant. Sean stood only a few inches taller than Selah but they both had matching chestnut hair and blue eyes, though currently his eyes were sparkling with mischief. Anyone who knew Sean understood he was trouble with a capital *T*. He batted his eyelashes at her now with his stupid you-gotta-love-me smile and his arms loosely crossed over his chest.

Selah glared at him, then yelled down the hall. "Mom!? Did Sean ask about going over to Daniel's tonight?"

Elizabeth yelled back. "Yes, Say, but I told him to be back before ten!" Selah had a feeling her mom was only trying to disarm her with the use of her nickname. Acting unmoved, Selah walked with a huff toward her mom's room. Selah began her question before reaching the bedroom door. "I'll make sure to remind him, but can't he just walk?"

Elizabeth let out an exasperated sigh.

As Selah walked into her mom's room, she noticed the dark circles under her eyes, and immediately felt shame.

"Selah, you have that car so you can help with your brother's transportation, so please just take him." Elizabeth's face pleaded for Selah to cooperate. "I will be back home in an hour or so. I have to head back to the office."

Selah turned around to leave, defeated. "Fine." She controlled her annoyance till she reached the living room, then rolled her eyes at the sheer ridiculousness of being her brother's chauffeur and the fact he was standing there shaking her keys.

UGH! He needs to get his license already!

"Okay, I am taking you, but you heard Mom, back before ten. Do you have a ride?"

"Yeah, yeah, don't worry about it," he said with a laughable New Jersey style accent.

They hopped into Selah's beat-up 1980 Oldsmobile Cutlass. To some people, Selah's car looked like a mess on wheels, but to Selah it was her pride and joy. This beast of a car continued to keep them safe; being built like a tank helped, but it often ate a hole in Selah's pocket. Sean never helped with gas; thank goodness Mom did, or they would be going nowhere fast.

Elizabeth worked long hours as a district attorney. She, unfortunately, had to take on even more work after their dad passed away, only to end up dealing with this kind of nonsense, like tonight. Whenever Sean and Selah bickered like this, Selah felt like an ingrate. Selah appreciated her mom's hard work. She understood giving her freeloader of a brother a ride was the least she could do, even with his pompous attitude.

Selah turned down the corner toward Daniel Lawson's house. It happened to be tucked into a subdivision not far from their house. His parents were not home this weekend. That happens often when your parents are well off and travel all over the world for mission projects.

Thankful the car trip was a fast one, Selah pulled up to Daniel's. Sean jumped out and turned to lean on the door. "Bye, Sis, see ya later! Also, go chill. You're practically atomic right now. I will make sure to tell Daniel you say hi!"

Selah grimaced as he winked and walked toward Daniel's front door.

Good riddance!

"Have fun." Selah said while faking a smile.

Daniel and Selah had been friends since they were five, so they had some history. In fact, they dated shortly during their freshman year. After Daniel broke up with Selah, they remained friends, though they hung out in completely different circles. Sean obviously loved to get her goat, bringing up her only high school relationship so far does that easily.

Selah heard the ruckus from the house when Sean walked in. She remembered to pull out her phone so she could text Daniel before she drove off. *Please watch out for my brother, he doesn't need to get into any more trouble.*

Daniel was quick in response. *Sure. No problem.*

She replied, letting him know she was hanging out with Jaidyn tonight and that she would be home just in case something happened. She pressed Send and headed back home.

It had only been a few minutes since she walked in from dropping off Sean when the doorbell rang. Jaidyn never rang the doorbell; she was practically part of the family. Selah looked out the left sidelight by the front door. There Jaidyn stood with her glasses perched on the bridge of her nose, backpack slung over one shoulder and both hands gripping the cover of a huge medical book, her eyes skim reading at breakneck speed.

Selah opened the door and moved to the side as Jaidyn walked right past her.

"Why the bell?"

"My hands were full. I think I may have found something about the," she whispered, "glowing issue."

Since the day Selah came into this world, she had had an unnatural glow. The doctors believed it to be a rare medical condition or birth defect. Selah underwent test after test till her parents saw the toll it was taking on her. They accepted this difference and Selah did too. Though once she started school, others made sure to remind her of how different she was. The torment came through the names like "Glow Worm," "Light Bright," or "Glow Stick." The only upside to school for Selah was having a few friends who understood her. By the time she got to high school, most people had stopped caring about her weird phenomenon. Not Jaidyn though, she took it upon herself to find a cure for Selah.

Selah was sure the annoyance of her brother's social life had her skin humming with light and was probably why he'd told her to chill out.

"How about we just start with homework? I have so much to get done. Senior year seriously sucks so far!" Selah grabbed her stack of books and went to the kitchen. Not quite the "chilling out" Sean meant, but it helped to distract her mind.

Jaidyn followed her into the kitchen. Their living room transitioned right into the kitchen with an island. Selah set down her books and sat on one of the barstools.

Jaidyn set her book down but continued to read, glancing away for only a moment to grab a snack from the cupboard.

"Give me some of those." Selah grabbed the box of wheat crackers Jaidyn picked out.

Jaidyn laughed and looked back at her book. "Where is Sean?"

"Guess?" Selah cocked an eyebrow.

"Daniel's?"

"You guessed it."

"Why does he hang out with Daniel so much?"

"I don't know, but it is kinda good though. Daniel is probably the only decent friend he has besides Tony."

Tony O'Neal—another lifetime friend. Tony could understand Sean probably at a different level than Daniel because he also knew significant loss. Selah appreciated both Daniel and Tony for watching out for her brother.

"Yeah, I guess you're right." Jaidyn smiled and went right back to her book. Though she was a geek, Jaidyn embodied beauty. Long, wavy dark-auburn hair surrounded her, and her eyes were a magical blue green. Jaidyn had a classic style and her cat cat-eye glasses topped off the geek-chic look. Jaidyn was oblivious to her beauty nor did she seem to care what others thought of her. That's what Selah loved about her. She was herself, take it or leave it.

Selah began working her homework. Jaidyn joined in once she finished reading. When neither of them had to go to work, this was their typical night together. While they both dreamed of moving out of Gailton, they knew the only thing that would get them out of here was their brains and hard work.

Granted, Selah loved this quiet little town; smack dab in the farmlands of California, there just wasn't much here but the pungent smell of cows. At least in Gailton the people helped each other out, for the most part. The one drawback about small-town life was that everyone knew your business.

Jaidyn and Selah were hoping to move to the coast during college, maybe go to UC Monterey or even further south like, San Diego. The whole point of all their hard work was to get top grades so they could get scholarships, hopefully to schools outside Gailton's surrounding zip codes. They both hoped to move onto bigger things. At the rate life was going, Selah couldn't see those dreams coming true.

A half hour later, Elizabeth pulled up, after her run to the office. Selah heard her keys rattle in the door just as they finished up their first assignment. Elizabeth smiled at them as she walked in.

"I am going to go change, girls." She dropped her bags by the door. "Think you would be up for a movie when I come out?"

Selah thought of how hard her mom has had to work, and yet even when she was thoroughly exhausted, she made time to connect. Selah noted all the times she had done this over the past few years since Dad passed, and felt her heart swelled.

Jaidyn smiled. "Sounds like my kind of fun." Then she looked at Selah waiting for her to say something.

Trying to keep her emotions at bay, Selah gave a quick smile. "Sure Mom. We just have a bit of calculus work to do."

"You girls are so smart! I don't even think I could do basic algebra right now, my brain is fried." Elizabeth's voice trailed off as she continued down the hall and into her room.

❦ ✦ ❧

Finished. Selah slammed her book shut, and took a deep breath, and looked over at Jaidyn. "You ready for pj's and some air-popped popcorn?"

"Totally!" Jaidyn shut her school book too.

Selah prepped the air popper and headed toward her room. More often than not, Jaidyn would sleep over. She had clothes there in her very own drawer. Both of them changed while the popcorn finished.

"Okay girls," Elizabeth said from the couch, remote in hand. "Comedy, romance, or action?"

After shaking a fair amount of garlic salt on the popcorn, Selah plopped on the couch, then Jaidyn followed suit. "Romance!" they said in unison, and they both reached into the large bowl grabbing a handful of popcorn each. They chuckled at themselves as Elizabeth scrolled through the list, then started a classic tearjerker on Netflix. *The Notebook* started playing.

It wasn't long before Selah heard the soft sleepy breathing coming from her mom's direction. Selah met Jaidyn's eye and pointed at her mom; both of them laughed quietly as Selah got up to cover her with a blanket. Instinctively Selah looked at the clock. "Crud, it's eleven o'clock!"

Alarmed Jaidyn asked, "What's up Say?"

"Sean was supposed to be home by ten!" Selah forced a panicked whisper, which came out sharper than she intended. She didn't want her mom to wake up. Selah began walking to the other room quietly and motioned for Jaidyn to join her.

Once in the room, Jaidyn said quietly, "Maybe his ride is late or he lost track of time." She had to love Jaidyn's optimism, but it didn't ease Selah's fear.

"Maybe you're right," Selah said, but before she could think any more about it she was dialing Sean's cell.

No answer.

Oh my gosh, Sean really!? Answer your phone.

She dialed Daniel's number, and it went straight to voicemail. Then she called Tony. If he didn't answer she was going to drive right over there. To her relief Tony answered.

"Hey Say, what's up?" His voice was drowsy and a bit thin.

"Hey Tony. You're at Daniel's, right?" Panic rose in her still.

"Yeah."

"Is Sean still there?" Selah interrupted before he could say another word.

He cautiously answered, "Naw, he left over an hour ago when Marcus came and picked him up."

"What? With Marcus?" Marcus Powell was the last person her brother needed to be around.

"Yeah… Sean should totally be okay he was sober when he left. Besides, what's the worst that could happen?"

CHAPTER 2

SEAN

Marcus could be a creep to most people. Tonight, however, Sean let it pass since Marcus was getting him into AfterBurn. This club was the place to be; everyone came here, mainly because it was the only fun place to be in this hick town.

Sean had lived here his whole life. He dared to dream that to one day, he too, would get the heck out of this isolated city. Sean only found shadows and sadness in this Godforsaken town since his dad passed away. All he wanted to do is get away from it all!

Marcus walked past the bouncer casually, tilted a brief nod of his head as Sean followed. The bouncer paid no attention as he passed. *That was easy.*

Judas Price, Marcus's friend, owned the joint. Okay, so he managed it, but still. Marcus and Judas were like brothers. Sean used to actually think they were. That explained why with Marcus by his side, Sean was able to slither past all the people waiting desperately to get inside. Sean's heart raced, excited to get inside and start this party off right! Sean knew his sister was going to be mad that he left Daniel's, but he was so done with having a babysitter. Plus, it was a bit of a snooze fest. Sean was looking for something a little more effective to take his mind out of this world, and playing video games at Daniel's house with a bunch of dudes wasn't cutting it.

AfterBurn had been decorated like a goth-glam nightclub. All black leather and chandeliers with blood-red fabric draped from the ceiling; it actually looked a bit ritzy for this town. It sure attracted a crowd though. Tonight, the DJ was playing thrashing electro-industrial beats. Marcus sat down in a booth surrounded by sheer red curtains. Sean followed. From the office door popped Judas, and he waltzed over. This guy had serious vanity issues.

"Marc, who's this?" Judas shot a quick glance in Sean's direction. Judas always acted smooth. In fact, so smooth he forgot Sean's name for the hundredth time.

"Sean, Sean Moore. We have met a few times before." Smiling, Sean put his hand out to give Judas a handshake.

Judas only looked at his waiting hand, then smiled like a snake. "Oh yeah, you're Selah's brother."

How could Judas know Selah and not remember who Sean was? His sister was always too busy hiding, doing homework or working, to party with the likes of these people. "Yep, that's me." Sean gave a quick nod, and put his hand back in his pocket.

As far as creeps went, this guy definitely was one. Judas Price, pretty-boy extraordinaire—rolling in the dough and constantly surrounded by beautiful women. Which was too bad, because his current girlfriend, Anne-Marie, was hot stuff. Judas personified the word *jerk*, while Marcus was at least chill, for the most part. Sean had heard rumors about Marcus for a while, and they had been to many of the same parties. So, he knew Marcus was the one with the hookup.

As if he had done it a million times, Marcus laid out a few lines of crushed Doxy. Sean heard this stuff was killer; a trip you'll never forget. Sean watched Marcus take the first hit. He inhaled a whole line, and without even stopping, inhaled another. This guy was fierce! Marcus caught Sean's eye. "Your turn, bro!" He handed Sean a rolled-up hundred-dollar bill. Sean couldn't remember when he had last held that much cash, and here Marcus was using it to snort Doxy!

Well, shoot, I guess I am too.

Sean took the hit. In an instant he felt electricity shoot through every inch of his body. He was floating, or his soul was; the room spun, and his heart raced. *Is that my heartbeat? Woah!* Sean searched the room for something to ground him, and his eyes caught on Judas, but Sean's eyes went wide when he saw horns. Judas looked like a goat-man.

Everything suddenly got really hazy, then crisp, then hazy again, as his eyes tried to adjust. Sean gawked as blood ran down the walls.

Marcus turned to face Sean. "You okay, man?" Marcus's face flashed, revealing red-pocked skin, rotting teeth, and onyx-black eyes. Sean felt the horror rising up inside him. Then he heard Judas.

"Dude, how much did you give him? That batch is mixed with demon blood man! Are you an idiot,

Marcus? Luc is gonna have my hide if he drops dead in this place!"

Sean's mind was trying to catch up with the spinning, which only made him dizzier. When Judas turned, Sean saw those curled horns, only they were coal black, sprouting from his temples; his skin blood red and scarred like Marcus's. Sean stopped himself before a scream welled up in his chest. He needed to move and get out of here.

Sean wobbled—holding the table wasn't helping. This high stopped being fun two seconds after he snorted that stuff. *Lord help me!* His grip tightened on the table as he heard voices rising; all he could make out was something about their boss Luc Vega and some plan he had.

Sean could hear his sweat dripping from his forehead. *How can I hear my own sweat?* He tried in desperation to walk away, but with jelly legs and little coordination like a newborn fawn, he wasn't moving fast enough.

Judas yelled at Marcus, "Listen, you imbecile, I am not going to let you ruin our plans so you can toy with these humans!" In came Marcus's other friend, Sean forgot his name—Sin, Sing, Sang... he couldn't remember. He walked up to Judas and told him to back down. In one swift movement, a movement Sean's befuddled mind saw with slow-motion trails, Judas ripped out the dude's heart.

What the Hell!!

Sean shook his head. There was no way he just saw Judas rip out some dude's heart. He looked again, as blood trailed down Judas's elbow, and he dropped the organ with a wet thud.

Crap! I need to get out of here!

Sean stumbled his way towards the exit.

Get out! Get out!

His mind screamed at him. Sean slowly started to sober up when he barreled through the exit and into the cold night air. He used all his focus to get home, which luckily, was only a few blocks away. He ran as fast as his clumsy feet would take him, but Sean couldn't shake the feeling of being chased. He kept looking back, and though no one was chasing him, he continued to run till his feet hit his driveway.

• CHAPTER 3 •

SELAH

Jaidyn and Selah threw on slippers and got ready to go look for Sean. Selah swore if he was passed out on the floor somewhere she would kick him, hard.

Ugh!

Sean had totally stopped caring about life since Dad died. What made Selah mad was that he acted like no one else in the family was hurting. They had all lost Dad. This destruction of his seriously had to end. Selah kept praying for God to intervene, but it scared her to think that maybe God had washed His hands of Sean. Mom used to say God loves you even in the darkest moments of life, but Selah could only wonder what God was thinking about Sean right now?

Just when Selah finished getting her slippers on her feet, she heard the front door open. Her feet carried her quickly across the room to Sean. When Selah saw his face, her desire to punch him disappeared. He looked shaken to the core.

"What happened to you Sean? You were supposed to be home like an hour ago!"

"Say." He seemed relieved. His tone, however, carried so much distress. He was freaking her out.

"Say, listen, I just went to go have some fun without your bodyguards watching me, but I'm sorry, seriously! I am so, so, sorry." He began to cry—shaking and crying. The last time she had seen him this tore up was three years ago. She stood back and got a good look at him, pale as a ghost, sweating like a pig, and...was that blood on his shoes?

"Sean, where were you?" Her domineering older sister tone came out without warning.

"AfterBurn."

Goosebumps raised all over her arms at the mention of AfterBurn. This club had been bad news from the beginning; nothing but drugs, drunkenness, and depraved things happened in that place.

"Sean, why are you bleeding?"

He looked down. "I have no idea."

Jaidyn was already by Sean's side, trying to coax him to the bathroom so they could clean him up. Selah tried to wrap her mind around what could have possibly happened to Sean; she tried to tame the protective and revengeful thoughts roaring through her head.

Jaidyn ushered him to the bathroom just in time because he puked, luckily in the toilet.

Sean started crying again. Jaidyn rubbed his back, soothing him, calming him down. She was like that with anyone and everyone, but she was always more tender and empathetic to Selah's crazy brother.

"Go get a cool washcloth," Jaidyn demanded as she was in deep concentration, doing her doctor thing.

"Sure, anything else?" Selah swallowed down her frustration, trying to be helpful.

Sean retched again.

"How about some water?" Her eyes, locked with Selah's, showed her deep concern for Sean. Selah loved Jaidyn. She was always filled with mercy while Selah was trying to keep from strangling, hugging, and then punching her brother. Selah needed to know who had done this. Her brother always seemed to get himself into some kind of mess, but this seemed far more serious.

Selah worked her way around the kitchen getting water and grabbing some crackers in case Sean decided he was hungry after all that heaving. She went back to the hallway closet and got all the supplies Jaidyn needed.

Jaidyn was still rubbing Sean's back. He seemed quite a bit calmer. Selah handed Jaidyn the washcloth, then set the crackers by the sink. Sean sat on the floor his knees pulled up to his chest, arms resting on his knees, his hands pulling back his hair. Selah reached out and handed him the glass of water.

Jaidyn being just as curious as Selah asked, "Sean, do you think you can tell us what happened?" She gently touched the wet washcloth to his forehead.

Sean looked up at Selah. "Say, promise me you won't get mad."

"Just tell me. I am beyond mad now; I am concerned. Tell me you wouldn't flip if I came into the house late looking like you?"

Sean nodded. "Okay, I'll give you that." He paused to take a deep, calming breath. "Tonight was not supposed to end up like this. I only left Daniel's house because I wanted to have fun. Marcus and I went to AfterBurn, and I ended up trying Doxy for the first time."

"What the hell were you thinking?" She frustratingly kept her volume low so Mom wouldn't wake up in the other room.

"Say, calm down," Jaidyn said in a gentle tone. It must have been her presence because no part of Selah wanted to calm down. Jaidyn looked Selah in the eyes, and the raging flame in her died down a bit. So did her glow, which seemed to burn brighter when emotions ran high.

"Okay, Sean, continue." Selah took a steadying breath of her own.

"So, when the drugs hit, everything went crazy. Blood dripped down the walls, Judas and Marcus looked like some kind of monsters from a horror movie, and then something happened." He paused and looked at his hands. "Judas ripped some guy's heart out!" His tone was shrill at the last statement.

"The drugs must have hit you hard, huh?" Selah's disbelief gave her away. He must have been hallucinating.

"Tell me how I got blood on my shoes, Say!?" he growled at her.

"I have no idea, but that story seems a bit farfetched, don't ya think?"

With full assurance, he looked her square in the eye. "I swear on everything that was good about Dad. I am serious!" Now he had her attention. He would never swear on Dad like that if there wasn't some truth to what he was saying. He loved Dad too much. Selah looked at Jaidyn. She gave Selah a brief nod. She knew it too.

"Sean, I believe you, but I really should see this for myself."

He got up in a frenzy and grabbed her shoulders, fiercely looking into her eyes, his grip was too tight. "Don't you dare! I couldn't live with myself if something happened to you. I am barely holding it together now! Please promise me you won't go to AfterBurn. Please!"

Everything in Selah knew she was about to lie to her brother, and she hated lying. She needed to find out what the heck was really going on in that place. If anything, she wouldn't do it alone. Closing her thoughts down even as Jaidyn's eyes read her like a book.

"Okay, I promise."

He relaxed and crushed her with a hug. In fact, he hugged her so long she had almost thought he'd passed out. Then he stepped back and kissed her forehead. She hadn't felt that brotherly affection in a long time, and her heart warmed, only to solidify the plan in her mind.

"Good." Sean gave an exhausted smile. "I think I could go to bed now. Please don't tell Mom, okay?"

That, Selah didn't have to lie about. The last thing Mom needed was more stress.

"Okay."

Jaidyn and Selah walked him to his room, not convinced he could put himself in bed without falling over. They watched from the doorway as he climbed into bed and turned away.

Jaidyn looked at Selah, shook her head, and whispered, "I know you, Say. You're not going to drop this, huh?"

"Nope."

CHAPTER 4

TONY

Tony continued to toss and turn, his body and mind a mix of restless energy, but Tony just wanted to sleep. His phone vibrated on his dresser, drawing Tony out of bed. With the way his night was going, it was more of a relief than a nuisance. When he read the name that popped up on the screen, he smiled.

"Hey Selah, what's up? Did you find Sean?"

"Well, he is okay now, but something happened tonight at AfterBurn and whatever it was, it spooked my brother. You know him Tone." He smiled when she said his nickname, but it faded as she continued. "This was different than any other time I have seen him messed up. I really need to find out what is going on over there before Sean gets hurt, but I can't do it alone."

Tony understood, and he would be glad to be of service, anything to get his mind off life right now, and if it meant spending some time with Selah, he would welcome it.

He remembered the day when her presence in his life felt more like home; it was months after she lost her dad, when he witnessed the pain in her eyes; he understood that loss, the deep inner turmoil and the strength it took to keep pushing forward. Her sigh of worry brought him back to the conversation. "You want to meet up and go over there tonight?" He checked the clock. "It's like 1:00 a.m."

"No, not tonight. I promised my brother I wouldn't go at all, so tonight is too soon. He would know what I was up to. Maybe next weekend or something?"

"Just let me know. Is Sean going to be okay? Should I come by?" He was concerned for Sean, but he was more concerned for Selah. This had to be tearing her to pieces.

"Thanks, Tony. He should be fine. I think Mom would trip if she found out you came over this late. Just keep an eye on Marcus and Judas, and try to keep them away from Sean."

"What exactly did Sean get himself into? Like really, just tell me." What was this kid thinking? Sean was like a little brother to him. Tony regretted ever letting him go with Marcus. Guilt hit him like a punch to the gut. "I am so sorry. I should have made him stay here."

"My brother is stubborn and makes his own bad decisions. No one but him can take blame. But I just thank God he is okay. He ended up taking that one drug, Doxy."

Tony groaned.

"I am worried about him, because I don't think he understands what he is getting himself mixed up in."

His hand smacked his forehead, slid down his face, then rubbed his temples. Now he really felt like an idiot. "That stuff can straight up kill someone!" Frustrated at Sean's stupidity, Tony shook his head and continued. "I will keep an eye out, no doubt, but make sure you pay attention to campus too, come Monday. Doxy floats around there like candy."

"I never pay attention to this kind of stuff, but you best believe I will now."

He had known Selah for as long as he could remember, for so long, in fact, only a few people called her by her nickname, Say, and he was one of them. He also knew that Selah was naive to the darker side of things and people. She had always been fiercely protective of her brother, but she really had no idea how bad it got around Gailton and Freedom High. "Well let's both keep our eyes peeled. You watch at Freedom and I will check AfterBurn before we go there together."

"Okay." She sighed deeply. "Thanks again, Tone, I appreciate your help! I'll talk to you soon." Even his nickname was rarely used by others, though every time Selah used it he felt bolstered, stronger; like she was the only one who was meant to say it all this time.

"Night, Say."

"Good night."

Selah was always optimistic, but since her dad had passed, her optimism had been mixed with a good dose of reality. She was strong and determined. On that day so many years back, when she lost so much, even wrapped up in her grief, she seemed to look ahead and never behind. He grinned.

He was just as determined to protect her and Sean before Sean ended up in even more trouble than he was already in. Well...going back to bed was out of the question; he needed to get out for a bit with some fresh air. Maybe checking out AfterBurn before closing wasn't a bad idea. Walking would do him some good anyway.

Even with the distraction of Selah's call, the flashbacks kept coming at him tonight. The crunching metal, smell of hot brake pads, squealing tires, his chest held tight in the grip of an unmovable seatbelt, glass shattering, blood, screaming, and sirens. He had been waking up in a cold sweat now for weeks. His heart restless, the grief so thick, he kept this nightmare to himself, unwilling to throw the misery onto anyone else.

Walking in the cool night air broke him from the misery as he breathed in its crispness. Sure, the air was forever mixed with the smell of manure, but it was a smell so familiar, it calmed his nerves. The tension in his body began to melt away.

Growing up in a small town, you learned the lay of the land. You learned the ins and outs; which side was the good side of town and which was not. These streets Tony could navigate at any time, day or night. When he wasn't walking the Gailton's streets, he was riding his motorcycle through the back roads, watching rolling green farm hills pass by. This town was a part of him.

He passed Lake View Park, which was a funny name for a park with no lake view. His mouth quirked a smile at the memories of Daniel, Sean, and himself trying to play basketball. Tony was far better at fixing cars than he would ever be on a basketball court. He would shoot the ball in the weirdest ways, knowing he would never make a basket, until that time he actually did make it; his back turned to the basket, eyes closed as he chucked the ball over his shoulder and... *swish*. Daniel and Sean never let him forget it. Crazy how this town that held so many dark memories of loss could also hold memories that made him smile.

He finally rounded the corner on Campanile Road heading toward AfterBurn, which was tucked into the back lot of Rite Aid. He had no clue what he was really going to do once he got inside. Tony's gut told him to go in and sit in the back of the club, to observe and take note of what he saw.

He turned down the back road, passing the vacant field that led to the parking lot. AfterBurn's all-black building with its lone red neon sign barely stood out from the dark field behind it. For looking so plain and drab on the outside, AfterBurn seemed to attract a good crowd; though when it was the only thing to do this late at night, it should have really been no surprise.

Tony was sported his usual attire of jeans, band graphic tee—tonight's being Van Halen—and his black leather motorcycle jacket. He played it cool as he stepped up to the door. The line was short, given that the club closed in little less than an hour. When he made it to the door, the stone-faced bouncer didn't look like he was up for any humor. Tony asked, "Are you guys still letting people in?"

This guy was not someone you would want to meet in a back alley. Maybe it was the angry scowl, scars on his shaved head—a long one above his right eyebrow—and his body was made of taut muscle like an MMA fighter, with the tattoos and attitude to match. The snarl on his face right now would certainly make Tony think twice before picking a fight with him.

"Yeah...ID?"

Tony pulled out his wallet, trying to lighten the mood. "I promise it's real." He handed over his ID to "Sunshine." Tony smiled as the name popped into his head, but he decided to keep that name to himself.

"Real enough. Go inside at your own risk." The bouncer grinned, but Tony could have sworn something flashed in the guy's eyes. Too early to get suspicious; he wasn't even inside yet.

He walked past the main curtains into the mayhem. Dizzying red lights flashing everywhere. The interior was far more extravagant than the outside, with black and red leather alternating booths lining the back wall. Round mirrored coffee tables for drinks sat in the middle of the booths, and above each booth black chandeliers radiated red light. There was a matte black dance floor with the DJ booth on one end; the three other sides were surrounded by tall standing mirrored tables. The place looked like an upscale night club. *What was it doing in this little town?*

Tony sat in one of the far dark corners. The music was so loud he could feel the bass in his bones. Trying to hear anything in here would be a challenge. This cyber goth music was pretty hypnotic. The repetitive rhythm warped around Tony like a warm blanket. The beat would normally be energizing, but it made Tony want to drift off to sleep. He would have to remember that for the next time he had trouble sleeping.

Before the tiredness swept over him, a waitress came to his booth. She was dressed in all black, asking him a question that snapped him back to reality. Shaking off the haze, Tony asked, "What? Sorry, I missed that."

"What can I get you to drink?" Her smile was teasing. He knew most guys would find her attractive; she was tall and blond with blue eyes. Tony suddenly realized who he was talking to, in fact, he kinda wished that he had hidden himself better. Quinn was one of the girls who incessantly picked on

Selah, and besides her cruelty, she was also quite dense. She had always made a point to flirt with Tony, and he always made a point *not* to flirt back.

"Yeah, thanks. Coke on the rocks."

Girls like Quinn, who were known for their partying, thought Tony's straight-edge lifestyle was a bore. Being straight-edge had its perks, all the hardcore awesomeness with no hang over or lapse in memory.

Quinn rolled her eyes at his request and walked away.

Tony looked around at the rest of the club; he saw hipsters smoking hookah, athletes drinking beer, a group of girls drinking fruity drinks, and all of them were underage. This place was a cop's dream. Kids he had grown up with were now all over this place getting wasted or high. For some reason, his anger welled up inside him. Why was this just happening and no one was doing anything about it?

Miss Congeniality came back with his Coke. "What are you doing here anyway?"

"Um...none of your business." He laughed, then took a sip of his soda.

Quinn tossed her hair to show that she couldn't care less and strutted over to the VIP section.

Wow, well, so much for customer service.

Tony noticed Judas and Marcus, who were swarmed by a group of inebriated young ladies.

Since Tony couldn't hear a thing, he watched as Marcus began doling out lines of Doxy. All five girls, including Quinn, took their share.

This was not good.

•   C H A P T E R   5   •

SELAH

The alarm on Selah's phone went off under her pillow. She tried not to wake Jaidyn, hoping to let her sleep a little longer. Selah stared up at the ceiling, and began to pray to God silently.

"Please, God." She inhaled and let her mind rattle on as she exhaled. "I'm scared. I can't lose Sean. I am not sure my heart can take losing him too. I miss Dad so much. God, I really need your help to keep my family from falling apart. Please, please, help me. In Jesus name, amen."

She did all she could to get up out of bed carefully, slipped on her slippers, then shuffled quietly over to the bathroom. Selah looked at herself in the mirror. *Oh goodness!* The dark circles under her eyes seemed to be getting darker. So strange though that the glow always remained. Taking in the aura around her skin, she tried to recollect all the times she had sworn she saw others glowing like she did. There were plenty of times she could remember seeing the same sort of aura around Jaidyn, but the more she thought about it, the sillier she felt. It couldn't be possible. It's not like it was contagious. She could only dare to hope that she wasn't the only one.

She shook out her whole body, shaking away the doubts and stress of all of her recent worries.

She brushed through her bedhead, wrestling her wavy brown hair into a simple ponytail. A simple layer of lip gloss and mascara was about the only makeup she ever wore. She quietly shuffled to her closet, picking out her favorite pair of jeans, a tank top, and hoodie. The greatest thing about fall weather in Gailton was the crisp cool mornings that turned into warm days and ended in brisk nights.

Selah went over and gently shook Jaidyn awake. "Hey, Jay! It's time to get up."

"Yeah, yeah, yeah, I know." Jaidyn had never been much of a morning person.

Jaidyn had stayed all weekend, which she did most of the time, though this weekend she stayed to help keep Selah sane. Jaidyn let out a huge yawn, looking like a lion with her messy auburn hair encompassing her, and yet somehow, she stilled look beautiful—one of the many traits Selah envied about her best friend. Jaidyn didn't have to try hard to look great; even with her unruly hair she always seemed flawless.

Jaidyn rubbed her eyes and reached over to the side table for her thick-rimmed glasses. As soon as she put them on, her geek-chic-self looked ready enough for school, except for her pajamas, which she probably could wear and no one would give her a hard time about it. Selah, however didn't need any more attention than she already got.

Selah was the dark beauty to Jaidyn's light yet fiery gracefulness. They complemented each other quite well. So much more than friends—a lot like sisters.

Selah got her schoolwork together as Jaidyn got ready. She was a flurry of cotton and chiffon. She quickly pulled on her jeans and then straightened her blouse. Jaidyn was quick. She put her hair in a messy bun, and just like that, she was ready.

"How do you do that? I swear I just don't get it."

"Do what?" Jaidyn said innocently.

"Get ready so stinkin' fast!"

Jaidyn shook her head with a laugh and grabbed her books and backpack. "Whatever! Come on, let's go. I really want to grab some coffee."

Selah had to wake Sean up for school, which wasn't as fun as one might think. Usually it took forever to get Sean out of bed. Mom was likely already off to work. Thank God her mom hadn't asked many questions this weekend because Selah really had no clue how she would have explained Sean's crazy story of what had happened Friday night.

Selah went headlong into Sean's room. "Sean! Get your butt up!" She grabbed the blanket and ripped it off of him. She yanked as hard as she could, only to discover a person-sized mass of pillows. "Sean?" She raised her voice as she headed to the hallway bathroom. "Sean!?"

"Say, you all right?" Jaidyn asked when Selah entered the kitchen. Selah looked around and retraced the weekends comings and goings to see where she would have missed Sean leaving the house.

Can't I sleep one night without having to worry about whether or not Sean is going to get himself into trouble? Where could he be?

She looked at Jaidyn, panic clawing at her chest. "You never saw Sean get up yesterday, right?"

"No. I thought for sure he was asleep. Why? He isn't in his room?"

"Just pillows. What am I going to do with him?" Selah was red from her chest to her ears.

"Maybe he actually went to school on time today?" Jaidyn asked, her voice full of hope. But even with her positivity, it sounded unbelievable. Selah grabbed her keys off the entry way table, frustrated with herself and her brother. At least he wasn't stupid enough to steal her car. Selah assessed her car as she walked out the door with Jaidyn in tow. She loved her beast of a car, and if her brother had stolen it, there would have been hell to pay. Though she would not put it past him if she wasn't always watching him like a hawk. Which made her even more frustrated with herself. She backtracked again and again, trying to see how she had missed him leaving the house. Selah tried to keep her teeth from grinding as she got behind the wheel. Jaidyn hopped into the passenger seat.

Selah let out a defeated sigh, "Jaidyn, what if he isn't at school?"

"Say, he always comes back. Always."

She was right, he always did. She wanted to laugh and cry at the same time. While that made Sean sound like a stray cat you couldn't get rid of, it also made her more nervous especially after this weekend's scare. Jaidyn looked her best friend in the eyes, reached over, and squeezed her hand. It was like Jaidyn could actually read her thoughts...

"We will find him no matter what." Jaidyn gave Selah's hand another gentle squeeze, and peace washed over Selah. If they had to, they would turn the city upside down looking for her brother.

"Okay," Selah said as she put the keys into the ignition, took a deep breath and put the car into reverse, then made her way to Freedom High. Their school was walking distance, but Selah would rather drive her car to school now that she could. It came in useful to tote around her friends and for when she had to work after school.

Selah scanned the neighborhood back and forth through her window and Jaidyn's, also checking her rearview mirror as she drove the best walking route to school. She was desperately hoping to see Sean's face amongst the other students meandering to school. She could see so many familiar faces but none belonging to Sean.

She spotted Daniel walking, his backpack slung over one shoulder, his head up, confidently waving hello and smiling at passing friends. Selah pulled up beside him and rolled down the passenger side window. "Hey, Daniel, I hate to ask, but have you seen my brother this morning?"

"Hey!" he said as he came closer. "Not since the party at my house. Why, what's up?" He squatted down to be at eye level with Selah and Jaidyn. He leaned on the passenger side door, but before Selah could answer he added, "Hey, Jaidyn."

Jaidyn said a quick, "Hi."

Selah continued. "He wasn't in his bedroom this morning. I'm worried about him. He tried Doxy the other night, then something happened at AfterBurn, and now he is gone."

"Wow, Say, I had no idea. I knew he was going out with Marcus. I just imagined they were going to the club to check out girls or something just as harmless. But Doxy? I'm sorry, Selah."

"I wish he didn't need a sitter twenty-four seven." Her shoulders slumped, and she looked to the car floor. "I just wish he would think things through." Daniel gave a sympathetic nod. She let out a sigh and asked, "Would you like a ride?"

"Sure!"

Daniel wasn't one to refuse a ride. She smiled then threw up her thumb toward the back seat, letting him know to hop inside.

"Thanks!" He smiled back brightly, waggling his eyebrows.

"Just get in already." Selah chuckled, shaking her head. For a quick moment, she forgot how desperate she was to find her brother.

Daniel opened the door. Jaidyn slid herself and her seat up a bit so Daniel could crawl in the back. Once he was in she closed the heavy door.

Selah continued to head toward Freedom High. Jaidyn and Daniel talked about the test coming up this week in their history class. Selah scanned passing faces once again, but it wasn't long till they hit the school parking lot. Selah parked her car, gripped the steering wheel with a white-knuckle grip, and secretly prayed.

God, please, please, please keep Sean safe.

● CHAPTER 6 ●

SEAN

The night he spent at AfterBurn left him shook, but tonight the silence in his room was excruciating. Voices plagued his mind.

How much further can you fall?

Why do you even bother?

You will always disappoint everyone.

Just get it over with.

His skin crawled with the need to leave. If he could out run these thoughts, silence them for a little while, maybe, just maybe, they would cease.

Sean pulled on a shirt he had flung on his chair earlier this week, not caring much if it was even clean. He checked himself in the mirror.

Looking good.

Sean was not going to wake up Selah. He didn't want a lecture or her worried eyes pleading with him to behave. So, walking was the only option this late at night. He checked the clock again. Midnight was usually not a good time for a stroll, but he didn't care.

Sean climbed out his window into the side yard, just like he had done countless nights in the last three years. Luckily, the street lights were working well tonight. Most the time, the dark streets gave Sean the creeps. Tonight, though, he found he didn't lack in courage, or maybe it was stupidity, he hadn't quite decided yet. He walked the next five miles to Marcus's house, constantly checking over his shoulder.

When Sean finally made it to Marcus's driveway, his mind was weighed down by his desire to be separated far from all his disappointment and pain. Doxy would be all he needed to get out of his head for a bit.

As soon as Sean's feet hit the walkway, Marcus opened the door and smiled like he understood some joke that Sean just didn't grasp. *Did Marcus expect me to come looking for him?* If Sean was really honest with himself, he couldn't care less if Marcus expected him or not. In fact, Sean didn't care about much right now but stopping the voices in his mind.

Marcus stepped aside and welcomed Sean in. Sean's jaw dropped when he stepped into the room. For a teenage drug dealer, Marcus seemed to live the high life, with a sixty-inch flat screen, two sleek modern black leather couches and every inch of the space immaculately clean, almost sterile like a doctor office. Sean wondered if he actually lived in this house.

Marcus sat on the couch in front of his glass coffee table and cut some Doxy right there for him. Sean hadn't even asked, nor had he given him any money, but hey, if this guy was giving out freebies, Sean wasn't going to question it.

Sean couldn't understand how it had come to this, snorting drugs off a coffee table with a guy as deviant as Marcus, but he shut down that thought and took a hit.

It didn't take long for the drugs to hit his system. In a matter of moments, he was oblivious to the world. Sean leaned back and enjoyed the rush. He felt like he was floating again. He stretched his left hand out in front of him and waved it around; blurring trails followed each fluid movement. He laughed to himself. This stuff was too good.

When he looked at Marcus, though, he saw that terrifying pockmarked blood red skin, and Marcus's feral eyes and hungry stare. *What the heck?* Sean rubbed his eyes and looked again, but Marcus was walking to the door. *Did the doorbell ring?* Sean tried to recall if he heard anything. *Man!* He shook his head but couldn't shake the blur from his mind no matter how hard he tried.

Sean looked up when he heard Judas at the door, but before he could even take in the horror of Marcus's face again, he blacked out. He drifted into sweet nothingness. Sean could hear voices hovering in his mind, not like the ones he was trying to wash away; these were farther away, they sounded deep, like growls and grinding bone. Before he could bring himself back to reality, he was pulled back again into oblivion. For the rest of the night he continued to slip in and out of consciousness.

Judas sauntered in and made himself comfortable. He eased into the sleek, cube-like black leather chair and tapped a dull rhythm with his fingers that were splayed on the arm. Judas looked at Sean with a mixture of pity and disgust, then set his eyes on Marcus.

"Marcus, you must stop giving out free samples to every Tom, Dick and Harry," Judas demanded in a low voice.

Marcus lounged in the chair next to Judas. He scooted to the edge of his seat and propped his elbows on his knees. Marcus leaned in toward Judas, holding his head up with steepled fingers. He pursed his lips and began to speak.

"Judas, think about it, the more these fools are hooked..." He gestured toward Sean. "The more they come back. Give someone a couple free samples, and boom, instant loyal customer."

Judas took in Sean's shallow breathing form. "You know Luc couldn't care less about one person getting hooked or not. He cares more about us getting caught by the "higher ups." He raised his eyebrows and implored Marcus to catch the point. "You are messing with a Chosen One's brother. Don't you think that is a little risky?"

Marcus got up and went over to Sean, lifted his arm, and dropped it. "Not at all. Look at him, he can't tell up from down right now. Once the Doxy really kicks in, and he begins to do things he never thought possible, he will sell his sister just to continue the high."

Marcus had seen it a few times before with those who survived. Addicts giving up everything to chase the high. With Doxy it was different. It wasn't just the high, it was the super human strength, numbness to pain, and the elated state of mind. The user was high all the time. Invincible. True, it was fake joy, nor were they ever close to being invincible, but none of these addicts cared. They gladly traded their pain for empty feelings and promises as long as the pain was gone, even if it was only temporary.

Marcus shook his head. If he had a heart, he would probably feel shame. He laughed to himself. "Pathetic right?" he said as he winked at Sean like he wasn't just talking about him.

All Sean could do was smile and drift back into delirium. Marcus encouragingly patted his cheek and went back to sit next to Judas. "This kid could be the key to help us actually take down the Chosen before they become a problem. If we play this right, Luc could very well move us up the ranks. Think about it, Judas, having our own territory to terrorize. Would be nice to not be under his thumb so much, wouldn't it?"

Judas and Marcus had no shortage of frustrations with being treated like peons by Luc. It had been centuries since they were formed, but they were still treated like underlings. This pet project of Marcus's could be the ticket to get them out from under Luc's constant scrutiny.

Judas stood up from his chair, buttoned his suit jacket and straightened his cuff links. When he reached the front door, he turned around to look Marcus dead in the eye. "Time will tell." He shut the door behind him.

Marcus knew this was his chance to prove his worth as a Greater Demon. They had been in this realm too long without freedom. They were always under the constant surveillance of Luc Vega, their Prince of Darkness. Marcus wanted his own territory to rule. He wanted to play without Luc breathing down his neck, even Judas, for that matter. However, until he could figure how to work it all out, this was the plan he had. He picked up Sean with one arm and slung him over his shoulder. Time to take out the trash.

• CHAPTER 7 •

SEAN

Sean shielded his eyes as he tried to sit up. The dampness from the wet grass soaked through his jeans. Vexed already and still squinting, Sean looked around, trying to figure out where the heck he was. Somehow, he'd gotten himself sprawled out on someone's wet lawn, and from the looks of it, not too far from his school.

He stretched out his jaw, yawning. Sean rubbed the sleep from his eyes, then ran his fingers through his hair. Every time he blinked at the brightness from the morning sunlight, he was met with sharp stabbing pain deep behind his right eye. Using his frustration as resolve, Sean pushed himself up and off the lawn, then dusted himself off.

Selah is going to kill me.

Last he checked it was Friday night. He remembered waking up once in his own bed on Saturday, that he had gotten up to use the restroom, but after that, fragments of memories scattered before him. All he knew for certain was his sister was going to notice he wasn't in his bed this morning. Sean shook his head at his own stupidity as he watched groups of other students take the back route to Freedom High.

Sean tried to blend in with the crowd while brushing off a few more blades of damp grass. After a few questioning glances from fellow classmates, he looked down at his shirt. From the looks of it he must have puked at some point while he was out.

Why do I keep doing this to myself?

Aggravated for losing control once again, he planned to go straight to his locker and remain undetected by anyone he really cared about. Sean always kept a change of clothes in his locker, for moments like these, in case he didn't go home the night before.

Seems like proper planning when you're playing the fool.

As he turned, heading toward the restroom to change, he heard his name. Sean rolled his eyes but turned to the familiar voice. Daniel had always been a good friend to Sean and Selah. Daniel had that pretty boy, pastor's kid vibe; it was hard to swallow at times for Sean, but Daniel was a good guy.

"Sean! Dude, your sister has been looking all over for you!" Daniel strutted over with a smile, but as he got closer his smile faded and his footsteps faltered as he took in how much of a mess Sean was. "Man, what happened to you?"

Sean looked down at himself again, disgusted. Sean played it cool—that was something he had always done well.

"Nothing a good changing and some water to my face won't fix."

Daniel looked unconvinced.

Sean shook it off and began to walk into the restroom. Daniel followed. "Where is Selah?" Sean asked, not sure if he wanted to avoid her or actually see her and hug her. Days like this, when he barely remembered his own name, he could use a hug from his big sister to feel whole if even for a moment.

"She went to first period with Jaidyn." Daniel looked concerned. "You going to be okay, Sean? I mean I could ditch and walk you home if you need some rest or something."

Sean thought he must really look pathetic if Daniel was willing to ditch school. "Nah, I'm cool. If I miss anymore school I will be graduating when I am twenty-five. Can you do me a favor though?"

"Sure."

"Don't tell Selah I am here yet. I want to talk to her myself, okay?"

"No problem bro. You got it. Take a nap in math or something. You look like you need it."

Sean half smiled and laughed. "Thanks."

Daniel left, heading toward his first period class. All these lies only made the irritation Sean had for himself worse. What was he going to say to his sister? *Oh, sorry! I went and got high.* Worse than that, what if she told Mom? If Mom ever found out, it would crush her. He finished dressing and splashed cold water on his face.

Sean walked back to his locker, chucked his nasty clothes in, and grabbed his math book. School was nothing to him. What was he going to do when and if he ever graduated? He wasn't a "master" at anything but disappointment. Would it even matter now anyways if he found something he liked doing? He didn't think so. So, like today he just played "school." Even with his mediocre effort, he was able to maintain a C average, of course, that was nothing next to his sister's A+ average. He knew he wasn't going anywhere any time soon, so like with everything else, he just stopped caring.

Sean waltzed into math class fifteen minutes late.

"Well, hello Sean. Nice of you to join us," said the smug Mr. Phillips.

Mr. Phillips was a nice enough teacher. His average height and lean muscular build didn't give him an overly authoritative look. "Everyone, turn to chapter 5."

Mr. Phillips wasn't your typical high school math teacher either. He looked like he just graduated high school himself. He was Japanese American with bright-green eyes and blue-black hair; most of the girls in the school swore he was a Calvin Klein underwear model. While Mr. Phillips did look like he could run circles around Sean, he wasn't all that. Sean might be a tad jealous because this guy made GQ seem effortless. Maybe one day Sean could be the hot substitute teacher at school. He laughed to himself.

Mr. Phillips cleared his throat, obviously annoyed at having to repeat himself because of Sean's distracting entrance. "Today we will be learning about quadratic equations."

Oh, Lord help me.

CHAPTER 8

SELAH

First period went by in a breeze. AP English always seemed to be one Shakespeare tragedy after another, and every Monday was another movie version of *Hamlet, Romeo and Juliet,* or *Macbeth.* Sometimes Selah and Jaidyn joked that it was because Miss Miller had too much fun on the weekends. Though Selah highly doubted that was the case, Miss Miller was the epitome of the crazy cat lady.

Selah's mind turned back to Sean's whereabouts. She searched faces in the halls as she and Jaidyn walked to their next class. Selah spotted Daniel.

He smiled and walked straight over to them. "Hey, I saw Sean this morning after we got to school."

She was sure her face showed her relief.

"He looked like a hot mess, but he was all in one piece. He did ask me not to say anything, but you know if it was someone I love, I would want to know. So, he is okay, but you didn't hear it from me."

"Thanks Daniel. You have no idea what a relief that is. I've been on edge all morning. I don't think Sean understands the anxiety he causes me."

Daniel smiled his most dazzling pretty-boy smile. "Well, I hope it has eased your mind a bit."

She smiled back at him.

"I was wondering if you want to go grab lunch off campus today? My treat."

Daniel's invite had a way of disarming her tension. "Sure, as long as I talk to Sean first. I will text you before lunch and let you know."

"Okay." He smiled at Jaidyn. "Jaidyn, you're coming too, right? And If Sean can stomach it he can join us."

"Thanks again, Daniel."

Selah gave him a friendly hug as the five-minute bell rang for them to get to class.

Jaidyn stared at Selah as they quickly walked to their next class. "You know when you're around

Daniel your glow seems to intensify. Have you ever realized that?"

"Um...no. That's weird." Her cheeks flamed. Gosh, could she not feel anything without having her glow give her away?

"Don't be embarrassed, just making observations. I thought you and Daniel were just friends since you broke up?" Jaidyn peered deep into Selah's eyes, trying to fish for the truth.

"We are. I can't help that he is attractive, and I once used to kiss him. Maybe that is why my glow gets brighter around him. He is a sweet guy, and cute, but we both know that is over."

"I wouldn't be so sure," was all Jaidyn had to say before she swooped into her math class right as Sean was gliding out. Jaidyn smiled and tucked her hair behind her ear. "Hi Sean, glad to see you're okay."

Sean smiled right back. "Thanks Jay."

Selah marched off. Sean quickly followed her, tried to catch her. She was obviously miffed with him. Selah rolled her eyes as soon as she saw him and turned to walk the other way. Sean finally caught up to her, grabbed her elbow gently, and coaxed her to turn around.

Her eyes gleamed with tears that she stubbornly would not let fall.

Not here.

Not now.

"Selah listen I know you're mad at me. Please let me explain." His eyes pleaded with her to just give him a minute.

Selah crossed her arms over her chest. "Explain," she said.

"I went out, looking for Marcus. It was almost like my body wasn't mine to control. All I wanted was Doxy. I must have gotten my hands on some because I can't remember all of Sunday. Say, I really don't know what to do. I know this is hurting you, but please don't give up on me."

Those words ripped into her heart.

"Sean what am I supposed to tell Mom? This will absolutely crush her if she finds out, and if she realizes I knew and didn't say anything to her—You really put me in a bad place Sean." She looked up at the ceiling in the hall trying to keep her tears from spilling over.

Sean grabbed her shoulders and pulled her into a hug. "Listen, Sis, I just need a bit more time. Also, I need you to stay far away from Marcus and Judas. I don't want you getting into this. I just need to find out what is really going on. I'm not crazy, and I will prove it."

He looked so sure of himself, but Selah could see this drug had its clutches on her brother already. She was afraid to give him any leeway. Sean was putting himself at risk. Selah knew he wouldn't be able to control his cravings for the Doxy. From what she heard, no one could.

"Sean, I will give you a week. Please try to stay clean. It's bad enough not knowing where you are, but not knowing if you are sober or dead in a ditch is terrifying."

Sean stepped back and looked into his sister's eyes. "I promise."

His words didn't ease Selah's mind one bit. She was going to have to keep an even closer eye on her brother, whether he liked it or not. She gave him a convincing smile. "How about you join Daniel, Jaidyn, and me for lunch off campus. Daniel's treat."

Sean lit up. "Well, if Daniel is buying, I want lobster."

"You don't even like lobster!" Selah laughed and punched him playfully in the arm.

"Yeah but Daniel has the means." He winked at her.

The one-minute bell rang. Selah quickly squeezed Sean's hand hoping to communicate she was with him in this, and hurried off to class. She still felt like she needed to keep him on a short leash. What would she ever do if something happened to her baby brother? She shivered at that thought and walked into her next class.

Sean breathed in deeply and slowly let it out as he watched his sister walk away. The heaviness of his continual mistakes seemed to weigh him down like an impossibly large chain wrapped around his neck, and it just kept pulling him further and further down into the darkness.

CHAPTER 9

SELAH

The lunch bell rang, and Selah began to walk toward the crowded parking lot. Freedom High let students have off-campus lunches, which usually meant a full parking lot every day at lunchtime. Selah scanned the parking lot, looking for Daniel, Sean, or Jaidyn. Instead, she spotted Quinn Myers and Anne-Marie Wilcox, both stunningly gorgeous and as lethal as poison.

Quinn was the fair-haired, thin and tall runway model. Anne-Marie was of average height, but she stood out all on her own with jaw-dropping curves, dark-brown hair, sharp green eyes, and a laugh that right now was grating Selah's nerves. They always attracted a group of willing boys to entertain them. Right now, Marcus, Judas, and a gaggle of drooling buffoons surrounded them. Selah dropped her head down and quickened her steps, desperately wishing she could be invisible.

Quinn laughed obnoxiously at something Judas said. Selah could feel Quinn's eyes on her before she yelled, "Well, if it isn't the Glow Worm herself! Heard your brother can't handle partying with the big boys."

Selah rolled her eyes and kept walking toward her car in the back of the lot, not daring to look behind her. She heard the distinctive sound of heels on concrete. *Oh God, please don't let Quinn come any closer.*

A hand grabbed her elbow and whipped her around, "Do you hear me talking to you?" Quinn looked at her in total disgust.

"Yeah, I heard you, Quinn. I chose not to answer." Selah began to turn back around, already done with this encounter.

"Hey!" Quinn maneuvered around her and got too close for comfort, staring face-to-face, keeping Selah from ignoring her. "I know your brother is getting the good stuff now. Watch out, Selah, he may wake up and realize he doesn't need you or your absent mother anymore. He may actually figure out who his real friends are."

Selah looked at Quinn like she'd lost her mind. "Excuse me?" Stunned, Selah shot back. "I'm sorry, who made you an expert on my family? Sean doesn't need friends like any of you two-bit, low life, sacks of human flesh. Leave him alone, Quinn. What have we ever done to you anyway?"

Quinn stood back, arms crossed over her chest, smirking to herself. "I have seen many families fall to the wayside as an addict chases a high. I don't believe your family is above those odds. Plus, Sean could have far more fun with me than he could ever have with his sister." She winked, turned on her heel, and slithered away.

Selah was relieved when she caught sight of Daniel and Jaidyn walking her way. Quinn smiled at Daniel and waggled her fingers at him in a pathetically flirtatious wave. Daniel gave a short wave back and pursed his lips when he saw Selah. "I assume the conversation you just had with Quinn didn't go too well."

"Oh no, we are total BFFs now." Selah let out the breath she had instinctively held in.

Jaidyn laughed as they continued to walk toward Selah's car. "What? How can she even take my place?"

"Believe me, there is absolutely no way on earth she would ever take that position from you."

"Phew! Had me worried there for a minute." Jaidyn shook her head, smiling as she opened the passenger side door and got in the back seat. "What did her majesty have to say?"

Selah got behind the wheel of the car. "She decided to tell me that my brother will ditch our family for the druggie battalion they have started."

Daniel belly-laughed, melting away the tension in Selah's muscles as she laughed too, Jaidyn soon joined in. Sean came up to Selah's side of the car and tapped on the window. Selah stopped laughing to turn the key in the ignition so she could roll the window down.

"You coming with us?" she asked.

He looked behind him. Selah watched as Quinn looked at him. "I think I might go with Marcus and Quinn. Can I just catch up with you after school?"

Resentment seeped into her words. "Sure, will you actually be home today? Or will I have to call the National Guard to search for you after lunch?"

Sean had the decency to at least look hurt. He reached in and squeezed Selah's shoulder, looking at her reassuringly. "I will be home tonight. We can talk then." He gently squeezed her shoulder again and backed away from the car as he said bye to Daniel and Jaidyn. Selah's shoulders tensed as she backed out, trying to keep her hurt and anger from affecting her driving. Selah looked in the rearview mirror and saw Jaidyn's eyes follow Sean as he walked to Quinn. The sadness on her face was hard to miss.

They pulled up to the local Taco Bell a few blocks from their school, which happened to be in the same parking lot of AfterBurn. Selah parked. Daniel and Jaidyn quickly hopped out of the car. As Selah got out she looked over at the empty lot at AfterBurn, she was relieved that Marcus's car wasn't there, meaning her brother wasn't either. Daniel opened the door and Jaidyn slipped in. He looked over at Selah, still staring at AfterBurn. "Say, you coming?"

"Yeah, sorry." She smiled at him.

Daniel beamed back at her. "Order whatever you want, remember it's on me."

She linked elbows with him as they walked up to the counter to order.

"Daniel, you really are the best."

They ordered their meals and sat down.

"Okay, so what really happened with Quinn?" Daniel was trying to be gentle about pulling out the details as he unwrapped his burrito and engulfed a third of it in one bite.

"Well, she of course started out with my revolting nickname and then commented on how Sean can't hold up to partying with the big boys. Then she continued to tell me how he will no longer have need for Mom or me once she gets her greasy hands all over him. Then, of all things, he decides to go with her... I am kinda tired of saying this, but, what is he thinking?"

Jaidyn sullenly picked at her taco salad. "Say, I really don't think he is thinking at all. Sean is better than all of them, and if he was in his right mind he would know that. Whatever he is messing with is really taking a toll on his decision making."

"Then it sounds like I need to get to the bottom of this and soon." She thought about the conversation she had with Tony just a few days ago when her brother came home so shaken from AfterBurn. She knew if anyone could help her get to the bottom of this Tony was the one.

Daniel looked serious as he caught Selah's eye. He finally swallowed his bite and warned, "Tread carefully. You know Judas and Marcus are in deep with Luc Vega. That guy is totally a kingpin from a bad mafia movie. Make sure to at least take someone with you."

Selah looked up at him a bit surprised. "I already planned on it."

CHAPTER 10

SELAH

Jaidyn had already gone to work. She had started as a veterinarian tech at Caring Hearts Vet Clinic last year.

Selah got dressed for her internship at the Gailton Police Department. She straightened her uniform, took one more look in the mirror, and headed to the precinct.

Selah had made the decision three years ago, when her dad was killed in the line of duty, that if she didn't move away for college, she was going to join the force after high school. She hoped to one day catch the man that killed her father, and with all that was happening at AfterBurn she was also determined to find out more about Luc Vega.

Her cell phone rang on her dash. Tony's face and name flashed up on the screen. She swiped to answer, then put him on speaker phone. "Hey, Tone, what's up?"

"Hey, I just wanted to call you and let you know that I did stop by AfterBurn the other night. Not much was going on that night, though it was near closing when I got there."

"You realize that's not going to stop me from checking it out myself, right?" She made it known, then heard Tony laugh on the other end.

"Oh, I know. What is it we are looking for anyway? Just the drugs? Because I can tell ya AfterBurn is chock full of them."

"That is only part of it. My brother came home with someone else's blood on him...and from what he described, there has to be some strange things going on there." Selah took a moment to keep her anxious imagination at bay. "Then, this morning, neither Jaidyn nor I could find him, only to discover he has actually been gone since Saturday evening. Whatever this drug is, it is just the surface. I mean, something about this whole situation is bothering me, and I can't quite put my finger on it." She was mad, not at Tony in any way, of course. Her biggest worry was that something awful would happen to her brother that she couldn't protect him from...or that their mom would find out before Selah could ease the blow. Selah's distress was credible.

"You know I am in this with you, Selah. Sean is like a brother to me. I would hate to see anything happen to that knucklehead. Maybe we can meet up on Friday to work out how we want to investigate this whole thing. How does that sound?"

Selah relaxed her grip on the steering wheel, feeling relieved. She rounded the last corner to the police station. "That sounds good." She paused with a smile, then continued. "Hey, stay out of trouble tonight I am patrolling with Officer Shields."

She could hear Tony's amusement when he replied, "I will be sure to stay off the streets! Have a safe night."

"Bye Tone. See ya Friday."

The phone hung up just as she pulled into the station's parking lot. She parked back by the dumpsters, in her usual spot, closest to the patrol cars. When she'd started this internship, it wasn't easy to keep from thinking of the night her dad died.

Eventually she shoved it away in a dark closet in her mind like most of her pain. The hardest thing to keep shut away was the pain she witnessed on her mom and brother's faces when they got the news. She promised herself she would prevent anyone from having to feel that pain, especially her family. *Never again*, she repeated to herself daily, an oath that at this moment kept her completely bound to Sean's livelihood. She would not let him get sucked into this world without a fight.

Selah walked into the station, silently praying that her service would make her dad proud. When she crossed the threshold of the Gailton Police Station, the front floor-to-ceiling windows with their clean, nod-to-modern design always impressed her. She greeted Kathy, the front desk clerk, then began making her way to the back office where Officer Shields was likely busy at work. She saw his office and could tell even from a distance that he was lost in deep thought as he shuffled around paperwork on his desk.

Selah was grateful to be under Officer Shields's leadership. He was a strong and brilliant cop, and when her dad was alive, he seemed to hold a high regard for Officer Shields. She shook the needling feelings of pain away, those haunting emotions that wanted to flood her heart. She would grieve one day, but today, as always, duty called. She set her shoulders as she continued to weave through the station; with each desk she passed her resolve returned. She finally reached Officer Shields's doorway. Her bright glow and smile were back in full force.

"Evening Selah, You ready for our ride-along tonight?" He assessed her from feet to forehead, checking her uniform and demeanor, confirming she was indeed ready.

"Yes, sir." She gave him a reassuring smile. "I just need to put my things in my locker."

"Okay, we haven't got a call yet, but the night has just started." His eyebrow lifted for a second, then he was looking back down at his paperwork. Selah took that as her cue to go quickly to her locker.

When she got to her locker she put on her name tag, then clipped her internship identification card to her belt, and locked the rest of her stuff up. She overheard a call come through Officer Shields's radio, before she reached his office. Another domestic violence call. This week seemed to have a strange

pattern between drug possession, dealer alterca-
tions, and domestic violence. Poor Gailton; their
little farm town was beginning to sound more and
more like a big city.

Officer Shields caught her gaze as he got up from
his desk. "Let's go, kid!"

●   C H A P T E R   1 1   ●

MICHAEL

Michael understood his time here on Earth was going to change the circumstances in this poor forgotten town, but watching as people continued to fall victim to the Fallen's tactics was really beginning to piss him off.

Michael, in an attempt to calm his anxious heart, thought of home. Heaven, its beauty and peace. He said a quick prayer and let the anxiety melt away, then the next call came into the station, another domestic violence call—third one this week.

The part of Gailton Michael was headed to now was plagued with gang violence and drug crime. Night after night, he saw the effects that evil forces played on this city, and each day he remembered that the time for training the Chosen was drawing near. He was grateful to God that Selah had signed up for the police internship program, making his job as her protector and trainer much easier. It was a matter of revealing the truth of their purpose and the truth of the Chosen's reality he was still wrestling with. How did you tell mortals they are blessed with supernatural powers to defeat an evil most people deny exists?

Michael pulled up to the corner of Elk and D Street with Selah as his ride-along tonight. Blue and red lights flashed over the scene as they pulled up. Officer Rivera approached Michael's patrol car. Rivera was a decent guy, bit of a hot head, but it was his partner, Officer Johnson, pinning a middle-aged Hispanic man down on the ground. Michael watched as he quickly cuffed him and helped him to his feet. For a scrap of a man, most underestimated Officer Johnson, but he sure packed a punch and was a barrel of laughs most days.

"I didn't do anything to her she didn't deserve!" She is nothing to me!"

Michael heard as he and Officer Rivera walked past the assailant. Officer Rivera began to brief Michael. "We came up to the house when he was pulling the woman by her hair. We asked him to let her go, and he continued to yell at her. Officer Johnson was able to tackle him to the ground while I slid in and moved the young lady away from him."

Michael gave a nod to Officer Rivera, then looked over at the victim, a young woman; she looked nearly half the perpetrator's age. She could have been his daughter, except she looked nothing like the assailant. She was crying, her hand covering one side of her face, her wavy blond hair covering the other.

The paramedics who had arrived on the scene started to treat and assess her injuries. One was taking her vitals and the other dressing her wounds. She winced when the paramedic wiped away the blood and applied the butterfly bandages to her eyebrow. Michael stopped at the railing on the apartment stoop, looking around. He could see the remnants of an ugly fight, the front door now wide open, a chair knocked over, a glass vase broken and scattered on the ground. He walked around, noting the look of the property, trying to give the paramedics a bit more time. Michael couldn't help but think that if Raphael were here this would go much faster.

Finally, with the paramedic's nod Michael approached the young lady.

"Evening, miss. My name is Officer Shields." He pointed to Selah, who was taking in the whole scene herself. "This is my intern Selah." Selah gave a cautious smile and a slight wave. "I wanted to ask you a couple of questions. I know you are in a bit of a shock, but hopefully we can get the information we need." He smiled gently as he motioned for her to sit down on the apartment's concrete porch steps. He sat down next to her, revealing more bruises as she grasped the rail to steady herself. She caught Michael's gaze and covered her face again. "Ma'am, how do you know this man?" He nodded toward the squad car the obnoxious man now occupied.

"He is my boyfriend."

Michael schooled his reaction to feigned indifference.

"How long have you been dating?"

"Awhile..." she looked away, trying to avoid both Michael and Selah from seeing her lying eyes.

"Listen, ma'am we can help you if you tell us the truth. Otherwise, you will just end up stalling the inevitable. Is this man really that important to you?

He seems to care very little for you or your well-being."

"I don't want to be arrested too." Her eyes pleaded for help. "I barely know this man. I met him online three months ago."

Michael looked into her eyes. His gaze tugged on her spirit. He had a gift of drawing the truth out of anyone. He hoped that Selah didn't notice the change in the young woman's demeanor.

"I met him at the local mall and thought we were going to meet for a movie. I was tired of my parents always bossing me around." Her lip began to shake. "He promised a fun time, and like an idiot I went for it. Sounds so incredibly stupid now that I say it out loud, but from that day until now, I have been trapped in this hell hole. I have been pimped out for the last couple months."

Once Michael pulled the thread of truth from someone's spirit, it unraveled like an old scarf.

"For the first month he treated me so good. Bought me new clothes, took me out to eat at fine restaurants, and made me feel amazing but kept a tight leash on me. I thought he was jealous for my time, seemed loving at first. It wasn't until he started inviting friends over to party and offering me drugs, and I would wake up unsure of anything that happened to me. One night I woke up with a needle in my arm and three people with me in bed and he was nowhere to be seen. It was after the 'parties' started, that I realized I wasn't in a relationship at all and that he was my pimp."

Michael took her hand in his. His heart ached like a father watching his daughter relive her worst nightmare. Michael tried to show her his deepest sympathy in his brown eyes, "What is your name?"

"Deanna."

Out of the corner of his eye, he could see Selah doing her job and dictating what was being said. "Okay, Deanna, I know this has got to be very difficult to talk about, and I know you have a family likely looking for you. How about I escort you to the station and we figure out what to do next? We will take your complete statement and contact your family."

"My parents are probably so mad at me right now!" The tears fell from Deanna's red-rimmed eyes, washing away trails in the blood that was already drying. She looked up at Michael with hope, her eyes pleading that he would tell her something different than what her mind was afraid of.

"I can tell you that if my daughter had been missing I would be so happy just to hear her voice. Once they know you are okay, we can have you guys sit down together with one of our social workers if it will help. I think you will be surprised how forgiving your parents will be especially knowing you are alive."

The tears continued to come as Deanna reached over and hugged Michael. Stunned, he gently patted her back as she cried. Selah's smile and spirit behind him radiated warmth that he was sure only he could feel. Selah had no clue yet of all the power her spirit held.

Officer Rivera looked at Michael and smiled. "We will meet you at the station and finish the report when we get there." Officer Rivera turned and began walking back to the squad car as Officer Johnson got into the driver seat. Officer Rivera got in the passenger seat and watched as Michael helped Deanna to her feet.

Deanna got her things from the apartment. She didn't have much—a small bag of clothes, her purse, and another pair of shoes. Then she joined Michael and Selah in the squad car. Deanna looked out the window and watched as the city floated by. Soon she would be reunited with her family.

Michael took in a deep breath. He looked over at Selah, who was still soul smiling. This was where his involvement with the human world had changed so much. He was used to fighting the spirits behind these acts of violence, lust, and greed, and all the other hellish spirits. Now he was in the mix of all the madness and chaos. He had pity on the humans, who seemed so ill equipped to fight. They often gave the devil a reason to believe he had the upper hand and had no idea they were even doing it. Michael knew otherwise and hoped that with each police case he encountered he could impact someone else enough that they would learn to fight for their life. Michael understood all along that this was why God made Selah his responsibility, because she wanted to touch the world in the same way. Michael vowed that he would equip her for maximum impact, not just against the Fallen and Devil himself, but to strengthen the resolve of her city.

• CHAPTER 12 •

MICHAEL

When Michael got home that night he was worn down and tired. His soul was heavy, like iron chains around his neck. He needed to see Raphael. He opened the door to his apartment to put his stuff down, then turned back out and closed the door. He headed down the hall; Raphael's was apartment was only a few doors down. He knew her shift at the vet clinic ended at 11:00 p.m., so showing up at midnight was no issue.

Michael rapped out a signaled knock. His soul lifted, and the heaviness he had felt became lighter as she approached the door from the other side. His sister, the Healer. Raphael was as beautiful and light as Michael was dark and intimidating. Their abilities were reflected in their human forms in only God's creative way, Michael all brawn and strength, while Raphael was radiance and grace.

Raphael smiled. "Evening, Brother. You look like you need some tea and a good soak in a hot tub. That long of a night, huh?" With a turn she began walking toward the kitchen.

Michael smiled and closed the door behind him as he followed her. She filled a tea kettle and put it on the stove. "What's on your mind?" she asked.

Michael was thankful for his sister. He smiled to himself, then glanced her way. What was it about her that made all the worries of the world melt away?

"Another night of watching Lucifer's influence on this city grow stronger. It's wearing me out not being able to fight him yet. I don't question our Father's decision, but deep down I just want to cast Lucifer out of this realm and be done with it."

Raphael's apartment embodied that light and airy feeling, filled with the comforts of what anyone would call "home," a place where you could kick up your feet and be comfortable. She sat down, and Michael watched as she rolled his words over in her mind. He could see her mental wheels working.

"Michael, it is hard for the warrior to watch the war building, to watch the events happen without being able to fight it right at the source. This battle is bigger than us alone. I know you know that, and this is your frustration talking, but the time is coming, Brother, I feel it."

And truth be told he did too. That's precisely why it was so hard to wait, as if they were at the crossroads waiting for a sign. He prayed that when the time came, they would do their part well.

Raphael continued. "Selah was with you tonight, right? How did that go? You think she suspects anything yet? It's been a couple months since she started the program. I'm actually surprised she hasn't noticed your abilities yet."

"Yeah. Selah was with me tonight... Raph, she is incredibly powerful already, and she doesn't even realize it, that's the most amazing part. For instance, tonight, we helped a young woman reunite with her family after she had been a sex trafficking victim for months. It was amazing. I could tell Selah was as happy about it as I was when I felt her joy rolling off of her like a heat wave." He sat back, sighed, then continued. "But, I know if I don't teach her soon to harness that power it will slip in times of distress, and God above only knows what would happen to anyone in her general vicinity. Our strategy will come full circle soon. The perfect time for revelation is coming. It's the way humanity's twenty years draws out to feel like eons. I am ready to fight."

The tea kettle squealed. Michael continued as Raphael grabbed two cups. She poured them both some chamomile tea and added a spoonful of honey to each cup.

"Do you think Jaidyn knows anything yet? I have a feeling they all know something is going on, but in their human frame of thinking they can't explain away their abilities."

Raph brought over the tea and turned to face Michael. She took a small sip of her tea then said, "You're probably right. That's why I think the time has come to break the truth to them and begin their training. Like you have witnessed with Selah, I witnessed Jaidyn do sutures tonight. The healing was nearly complete with the last stitch. That is dangerous. If anyone other than me saw that, there would be questions. But strangely, I too am incredibly

DAWN LEE DALEY

proud of her. As if she were my own child completing an impossible task."

This pride was unusual for them because Angels can't have children. But since each of the four Archangels were summoned to bless this region with Chosen Ones, the very children they blessed had felt like an extension of themselves. Michael understood Raph's words; he felt the same about Selah. She was an amazing human, but it wasn't her abilities as much as her warrior's heart.

He smiled at his sister. "I hear ya." Each of them knew the dangers of being emotionally intertwined with their charges. Michael continued. "But maybe this was part of our Father's plan, to show us his pride in humanity. They are, after all, His children and He smiles with joy at their greatness of heart and all the pain they feel He wishes to fiercely protect them from. It is so much easier to understand now." Raphael just looked at him with pure joy.

"Sometimes you surprise me, Michael. Even through the sands of eternity, you bring your strategic thought process to the understanding of empathy. This is why you are the chief, ya know." He blushed. Dang this human form.

"Thanks, Sis." He took his last swig of tea, beginning to feel the calming effect of the chamomile. "If nothing happens before Friday, I will see you at our regular meeting time." She got up to walk him out and embraced him before he left. Her hug was like the light of God; comfort, peace, and joy all wrapped in one.

"God's love be with you, Brother."

"As with you, Sister."

Michael let out a deep sigh, pouring out all his troubles. He squeezed his angel sister one last time, and he was back to the strength of a thousand men. As the chief of Angels, he knew he was nothing without his sister and brothers; all his strength, power and strategy were nothing without them by his side. He thanked God that he was not alone on this mission, because he couldn't possibly succeed without them.

• CHAPTER 13 •

SELAH

After the emotional high from Monday night's assignment at work, Selah was even more amped about her internship. At least it was way more exciting than the assignment she was supposed to be working on right now.

It had only been a couple days since her brother had ditched her and their friends to hang with Quinn, and in that time, she had tried to probe him with questions while casually trying to appraise whether he was okay or not. Strangely enough, since Monday he seemed healthier, almost happier, even content. Selah tried to relax a bit, but she still had an inkling that it wasn't time to let her guard down quite yet. She decided to be watchful but wary.

Selah folded the note she was about to pass to Jaidyn. Mrs. Vasquez was Freedom High's Spanish teacher and was Selah and Jaidyn's last class of the day. She and Jaidyn sailed smoothly in this class. Jaidyn was Mrs. Vasquez's teacher's assistant. Mrs. Vasquez never paid much attention to either of them because they were both good students.

Selah began to fidget, growing impatient. She wanted to have a real conversation with Jaidyn rather than pass notes.

Jaidyn kept teasing her about Friday night's plans with Tony. Selah scribbled again...

It is NOT a date.

SURE! was all Jaidyn wrote back.

Selah rolled her eyes and laughed.

Jaidyn was impossible.

Selah got up as soon as the bell rang and headed straight toward the door, shaking her head, still laughing with Jaidyn. Selah caught Daniel walking in their direction. Jaidyn must have too because her laughing stopped abruptly. It was hard to miss Daniel's bright, disarming smile shining on his nearly flawless face. Selah beamed back as he walked alongside them, heading toward the parking lot.

"Hey Say, I wanted to check on Sean. I haven't seen him since Monday. You seem all right, so I assume he must be fine."

"He was fine earlier today. In fact, he seemed different, like happier and healthier than I have seen him in a while. Surprising, since Monday he looked like he had been dragged through hell." Selah's brows furrowed in concentration as she tried to figure out how this could happen, unless he stopped taking the drugs altogether, but with the group he hung with now, that was highly unlikely.

Jaidyn piped up, "He could be well hydrated now. Sometimes that can help you look and feel better. Or maybe being around Quinn is actually helping." Jaidyn's voice nearly broke trying to get that last part out. They all looked at each other and laughed.

"Really though, I am shocked at how good he is doing. It's only been a couple days, but I am just happy to see him, I don't know, happy, I guess." Selah felt guilty for saying so, but in a way, she felt relieved seeing him act normal.

"That's great!" Daniel smiled and continued, "I just haven't seen him around school much."

Now that she thought about it, she hadn't either. She had given him rides to school the last couple days but had not seen him much during school. They were in very separate classes so that was really no surprise. She decided she would ask him tonight how his classes were going.

She asked Daniel, "Have you texted him or anything this week?"

"Off and on but got nothing back."

"Sounds like we may still need to keep a keen eye on my baby brother. Which, by the way, I greatly appreciate. You have no idea how hard it is to keep an eye on him by myself."

"Oh, we know," Jaidyn said, looking at Daniel, who nodded his head in agreement.

Often when anyone mentioned Sean, Jaidyn would get a faraway look in her eyes. Selah knew deep down it hurt Jaidyn to see him so broken as much as it did her. Jaidyn wanted to help and heal everyone.

Selah put her hand on Jaidyn's shoulder. "We will help him come back from all this."

Daniel with his hands in his pockets, tried hard to not look doubtful. Jaidyn, on the other hand had a spark of hope in her eyes. Selah was bone tired of all of this mess.

"How about we keep in touch with each other? That way we can know if he is okay. None of us need to worry if we each keep an eye out," Daniel suggested.

"Let's do that. I like that idea." Selah took a deep breath and felt her shoulders relax. "I am going to AfterBurn on Saturday with Tony to investigate a bit. My hope is to find out what is going on there. To find out what spooked Sean so badly."

Daniel looked like he just ate a frog. "You're going with Tony. To AfterBurn?"

"Yeah." Selah caught Daniel's expression. She quickly clarified what Tony and she would be doing. *Did he forget that he also suggested it?* "We are just going to find out what exactly is happening inside the club. From what Sean described it is pretty dark."

He looked at her like she was missing something but said, "Okay, sure. Just make sure to text me and let me know if you find out anything."

Before Selah could say anything else, Daniel said he needed to get home for something.

Jaidyn gave him a quick smile and said, "Bye, Daniel, take it easy."

He casually smiled back and walked away.

Selah furrowed her brow in confusion, then brushed it off and continued to walk to her car. She shouted back to Jaidyn, "See ya at my house, Jay."

* * *

The Moore house was always painfully quiet whenever Selah walked in the door. With Mom at work and Sean out doing God-only-knew-what. The silence was suffocating. Selah missed her dad most when the silence came. She missed him now more than ever, especially as her brother fell deeper into darkness. Her dad would have known what to do. Though, if he were here, none of this would be happening either.

She wasn't sure how much longer she could keep from shattering with the iron grip that grief had on her heart; it was getting harder to push away these last few months. She needed an escape even if just for a bit. Maybe Saturday would be a good thing, even though they were going to investigate After-Burn. The thought of possibly enjoying a night of dancing was a change of pace she could use. She laughed to herself as she tried to picture Tony dancing.

Jaidyn let herself into the house. Selah let out a deep sigh of relief at no longer being alone. Jaidyn strolled in and dumped her stuff on the couch then went straight for the fridge.

Selah checked today's mail. Just more bills. *Poor Mom.*

"You hungry?" The near empty fridge amplified Jaidyn's question across the room.

"Geez, I don't know if we even have anything in there. I can't even remember the last time Mom went grocery shopping."

"Well, hmm, let's see." She shuffled through a few things. She grabbed some Greek yogurt and blueberries, then went to the cupboard. "Jackpot!" She pulled out some granola and began making yogurt parfaits.

"So...have you figured out what you are gonna wear on Saturday? Have you even thought about it yet? I mean, AfterBurn may not let you in looking like that." Jaidyn looked Selah up and down, scrutinizing her apparel.

"What is wrong with what I have on?" Selah looked down at herself. Okay, maybe workout pants and a baggy sweater were not "club" clothes. "I don't have a lot of dressy clothes, Jay? Have you ever seen me go to a club?"

Jaidyn laughed. "Too true." Jaidyn pulled up a bar stool next to Selah and pushed a bowl in front of her.

"Eat, Say, then we will raid your closet. I think I can help you out." Jaidyn had a style all her own, no doubt, very hipster chic. Selah wanted Jaidyn to go with her and Tony on Saturday. She realized she hadn't asked her yet.

"Do you want to go with us on Saturday night? It could be fun. Honestly, I am kind of looking to have a good time despite the reason we will be there. I kinda need to let my hair down, ya know?" She could see Jaidyn contemplating it as she turned her spoon over to get the rest of her yogurt off.

"Sure! It could be fun. Not really my idea of a good time, but hey, I am all up for trying new things. At first, I thought maybe you didn't want me to go," she said as she continued to concentrate on her yogurt.

"What? Why wouldn't I want you to go? You're my best friend! Even if you didn't like it, I would probably still try to drag you along."

They both laughed.

"I just thought that maybe you wanted to be alone with Tony."

"Do you think that is why Daniel was acting weird when I mentioned it? You know, as bad-boy gorgeous as Tony is, I am pretty sure he is way off my radar. Don't you think? I guess I always pictured Daniel and I getting back together after sophomore year. But ever since he made varsity quarterback in junior year, I felt like he moved on." Selah couldn't overcome her feelings of being average, even though her whole life she had stood out because of her glow. She had constantly worked at trying to be unseen that now she really felt that way.

Jaidyn tilted her head, a smirk on her face an eyebrow raised. "Are you serious? I may be biased, but I am a good judge of aesthetics, and let me tell you, Say, you have it." She winked. "Saturday will be more fun than I thought." Jaidyn and her mischievous grin made Selah a bit nervous. They put their bowls in the sink and went straight to Selah's closet with only forty-five minutes to spare before work.

Jaidyn picked out some very random outfits. Selah was beginning to rethink this idea, but she tried on the second choice in the selection that Jaidyn laid out before her. A pair of faux black leather leggings and a dark-purple slack neckline halter top with built in black strapless undershirt. Jaidyn whistled. Selah began to blush and felt her chest warm.

Gosh, could I really pull this off?

Selah went to the full-length mirror in the corner of her room and shifted back and forth, taking in her full reflection, and was pleasantly surprised. Her curves must have filled out in the last year because this outfit had never worked before. She had kept it in the back of her closet, hoping that one day it would fit perfectly, and now here she was, gawking at herself.

"I told you, Say, stop doubting yourself. You are a total hottie!"

Selah smiled at her best friend's confidence in her.

The rest of their time together was spent on accessories and makeup choices, and ended with the decision that Jaidyn would indeed join her and Tony on Saturday.

CHAPTER 14

SEAN

Sean's gaze landed on Quinn, and he gave her a smoldering smile. Quinn, while stunningly beautiful, was entirely extraordinary, but Sean couldn't quite put his hands on what made her that way; almost like chasing sunlight, she felt illusive to him even as he sat next to her. The Doxy had his mind wrapped in these confounded thoughts. He shook them off as he reached over to squeeze Quinn's knee. Quinn turned, her eyes meeting his and kissed him.

They had come to AfterBurn because Quinn's shift was due to start soon. She broke away from the kiss and sprang from the booth, making her way to the bar. She took a shot of something red and swirling with light, then slammed the glass on the bar as she grabbed her apron.

Sean had tagged along the last few days so he could get his fix of Doxy from Marcus. The drug continued to numb his senses, but every hit he took seemed to make him feel stronger, more invigorated, even happier than he had been in years. He couldn't care less what anyone thought of him or how the drug may affect him negatively. He was just happy to have some sort of balance back to his life. For so long, he felt lost in a world of darkness, and now he felt confident, focused, and pleased, though he was still very much in the dark. Sean knew beyond a shadow of a doubt that his nightmares were behind a wall in his mind; he just prayed the Doxy would keep that wall from crumbling again.

Sean flinched and covered his eyes as AfterBurn's front doors opened. Blinding light filtered through as the crew trickled in for the night ahead. Sean scanned the room and watched the DJ as he talked to Quinn. *What does she see in me when she is surrounded by guys like DJ Tall, Dark and Handsome? or Uriel, the bouncer with his scarred eyebrow, tattoos, and muscles? That guy has badass written all over him.* If there was something Sean had a hard time with, it was definitely competition. The way Quinn looked at Uriel when she talked to him though, with her brazenness and full-on contempt, Sean felt he was safe. Uriel looked over at him with a pitied acknowledgment and nodded his head. Sean nodded back in mock kindness. *This guy thinks he knows, but he has no idea who I am.*

Uriel turned his back to Sean and started talking to the bartender as Quinn came back over to their booth.

"Sean baby, are you staying tonight?" She slowly straddled his lap and hugged his neck.

"Yeah, I will stay, but I should get home at a reasonable time to keep my sister off my back, or she will just be asking a bunch of questions I don't care to answer." Quinn smiled like the devil, and grazed her lips over his, and whispered, "Good." Then she kissed him deeply.

Sean grabbed her hips and kissed her again. A cough broke them apart. Sean looked up to see Marcus and Judas heading to the booth.

"Quinn, you're not a stripper, you're a waitress ya know." Marcus sneered.

"My clothes are on, you fool!" Quinn spat back, reluctantly getting up to sit next to Sean as Marcus and Judas sat on either side of them. There was plenty of room on this large U-shaped booth.

"You staying tonight Sean?" Judas asked.

"Yeah, not much else to do, but I have to bounce around ten or so. Why, what's up?"

"Nothing. Wondering if maybe we should give you a job soon, given how much you're hanging around here lately."

"Really?"

"You could be a bouncer with Uriel and his guys. But being you're like underage and all, I'm not sure how Luc will feel about it."

All heads turned to the front doors as Luc Vega walked into the club. That man demanded attention whenever he walked into a room. Sean was not fooled by the man's gray hair. Luc was all chiseled lean muscle and probably lethal if provoked. Luc's style, however, was a bit like a distinguished gentleman, making him look approachable, only if you didn't know of his legendary anger. Sean had witnessed it once the other night. Luc had found out one of the bartenders was shorting the register, and he dang near broke the guys arm as he escorted him out to the parking lot. Sean wasn't even sure what happened in the parking lot after that, though he imagined it wasn't kindness. Sean usually tried to stay under Luc Vega's radar.

"Luc," Judas called out, and sure enough, Luc began to walk in their direction.

Sean felt sick.

When Luc reached the booth he remained standing, and Judas continued. "Luc, what do you think about adding Sean to the bouncer's crew part-time? He is here most the time, and for now he can just work weekends since he is still a minor."

Sean began to sweat under Luc's assessing glare, trying hard to remain relaxed.

Luc asked, "Can you sprout some more muscles? I don't want some idiots thinking they can take you down to get in my club. If you can do that, then yes, I will add you to the crew."

Sean looked surprised; he was no wimp, but compared to the others on the crew he understood Luc's request. AfterBurn's bouncers embodied a "don't mess with me" vibe.

"Sure Mr. Vega, no problem."

"And just call me Luc, and don't get in my way. You can start this Saturday."

Sean nodded. "Sure thing, Luc."

Luc gave a curt nod to Judas and walked with purpose to his office. In that moment, Sean finally remembered to breathe. That went smoother than he could have imagined.

Judas smiled at him. "See now you have a reason to be here other than to see this sack of bones." He nodded in Quinn's direction.

"Whatever, Judas," she said. "You're just mad because Sean has what you want."

Judas cocked an eyebrow, looking skeptical.

Sean laughed nervously. Quinn got up and kissed him, then sauntered off, her hips swaying as Marcus, Judas, and Sean watched.

"You know that girl is trouble, right?" Marcus looked at Sean.

"Then why did you tell me to ask her out?" Sean laughed.

"Because you need her kind of trouble in your life, brother." Marcus grinned, raising his eyebrows suggestively. "You'll thank me later, believe me."

Marcus pulled out a small baggie of that finely crushed powder Sean desired so much, and handed it to him. Sean slipped him money. The music started, the lights danced as Sean divvied-up his hit and took it in one smooth motion. He sat back as the high washed over him like a fresh breeze on a hot day. He watched while people dressed to impress began to come into the club. Sean scanned the club again for Quinn. When he spotted her he smiled to himself. Yeah, he was happy.

• CHAPTER 15 •

SELAH

Another abysmal school day was over. When Selah got home she fussed over the house while her mind continued to go over what had happened today. She had spotted her brother at school with his arm draped over Quinn's shoulder, both of them laughing with Marcus, Judas, and Anne-Marie. Selah scrutinized Sean's every move, trying to see if the drug use was getting worse. What she saw instead confused her. Sean was of picture perfect-health. He was really looking better as each day passed. She was disturbed by how happy he was. She had been praying to see him smile like this again. The knowledge of a drug dealer and a vamped-up bully making him smile again crushed her. Maybe she had been going about it all wrong. What bothered her even more was how Sean seemed to completely forget what had happened to him just last week. That night he came home he was terrified of Judas and made her swear to stay away from them, yet here he was hanging out with them.

Selah stopped scrubbing counters for a moment. She looked around realizing how much cleaner the house became when she was feeling frustrated. She stood back to look at the great room, which contained their living room and merged right into the kitchen. She smiled with approval at her work, then went to change. She hoped not to smell like a janitor when Tony showed up. Selah was incredibly thankful that he was still willing to participate in this crazy idea of investigating AfterBurn. Selah, however, was really nervous they would find nothing, and she would end up looking foolish while her brother continued to slip further away. Selah prepared her heart for that possibility.

Once she freshened up, she got out some snacks and soda. She looked at the soda fondly, thinking about how Tony had chosen a straight-edge lifestyle. When people first saw him and his roguish appearance, they were shocked to find out his choice. Even

Selah was at first, until she found out why; his parents had been killed by a drunk driver. Selah imagined Tony as a child, sitting in the back seat watching his parents die. How traumatic it must have been to see that and be the lone survivor.

Selah wished her brother would go straight-edge, in all honesty, especially after the way their dad had been killed. That day, which she tried often to forget but would forever be etched in her mind. She stopped the thought train from derailing; the silence was getting to her again. She took a deep breath and let it go.

Tony would never forget the day his parents died. She saw it written on his soul like she could see it on her mother, brother, and even herself. She understood why Tony vowed to himself to stay away from intoxication, because he never wanted to lose control or at the very worst, take someone else's life. He was strong in his conviction. It was quite an admirable thing, and it was an honor to his parents and to himself.

Selah turned toward the front window, the rumble of Tony's motorcycle grabbing her attention. She glowed brighter. When he pulled to the curb she watched as he dismounted and headed toward the front door.

He really is intoxicating all on his own. Her cheeks burned at the thought just as Tony knocked on the door. She calmed herself, hoping to calm her glow too, as she put her hand on the doorknob. She opened the door with a smile.

"Hey Tony! Come on in." She stepped aside as he walked in and caught herself staring again as he passed. She was in trouble. She felt heat creeping up her neck to her cheeks again. Tony set his helmet on the entryway table and shucked off his leather jacket, quickly turning to face her. Selah tried to convince herself the sparkle in his eyes was from the ride here, not at seeing her.

"Here I am, now what do we do?" He winked at her.

Selah swallowed down the lump in her throat, then said, "Thanks for coming by tonight. I am actually really confused about Sean and what's been happening this week." Heaviness gripped her as she sat down on the couch. She grabbed one of the sodas off the coffee table. Tony did the same, then sat back to face her as he grabbed a handful of pretzels.

"What do you mean?" he asked. "How bad off is he?" Concern swept over his face as he narrowed his eyes in thought, then he popped a pretzel in his mouth.

"Sean was frantic the first night he came home from AfterBurn, like I told you when I called, but if you could see him today you would think I made the whole thing up." She sighed. "He is looking better than he has in years and has been on Quinn's hip since Monday. I assume they are officially dating.

"What confuses me the most is how absolutely upset he was when I talked of going to AfterBurn myself to find out what was up because he begged me to stay away, yet he is there all the time now. I can't tell if he keeps slipping further into the mix of it all or if it was just the drugs that night. I mean, it's weird. He looks good now, like sober and...happy." Selah wrung her hands together. "I just don't know, Tone, something feels off about it all." Selah knew how unsure she sounded, but Tony reached over and squeezed her hand with a reassuring smile.

"That's what we are going to find out then—if Sean is okay or if there really is something deeper going on. I have heard of some drugs making people seem better for a while till the addiction really starts taking over. Though my hope for Sean is that he is okay. Him being with Quinn is not good news though. I remember when you were a freshman with her and Anne-Marie, and I can tell you from personal experience both of them are menaces. I even would bet that Anne-Marie is some kind of witch or something. She once broke up with one of my friends—not sure you remember Donny? Well, he cheated on her, mainly because he was too terrified to break up with Anne-Marie. He had been playing on the basketball team at the time but was benched and later had to quit because the nerves in his legs kept giving out on him while he was playing. It wasn't long after when he found a voodoo doll under his bed. He was majorly creeped out and destroyed it. Sure enough, he tried to play basketball that weekend with some of the guys from the team, and he was back to his old self."

Selah's jaw dropped in horror.

Dear God, what would happen to her brother?

Tony continued, squeezing her hand again. "Say, listen, I promise you I will do all I can to keep my eye on your brother when he isn't at school and that will be a lot easier now..." He paused for a moment. "Since I got a job as a bartender at AfterBurn."

Selah stopped him. "What!? Is that something you even want to do? How does that fit in with your straight-edge lifestyle? Don't mess up your vow just for the sake of my stupid brother."

"I don't have to drink for the job, so in essence it's fine. Granted, the last thing I want to do is contribute to someone else's drunken state, but as bartender I can cut people off and send them home in a cab. So, I feel like I am doing a bit of a public service really." He smiled at her warmly, squeezing her hand yet again. She suddenly realized he had been holding it this whole time. "Plus, what better way to keep an eye on your brother. He just got a job there as a bouncer ya know." He looked intently at her, hoping she did indeed know already.

Selah was instantly furious, dropping his hand as she got up to pace the living room.

Tony watched her with concern.

"You have got to be kidding me! How is that even possible? He is only sixteen!"

"Luc is letting him work part-time on weekends, so he can get away with hiring a minor, plus he isn't serving alcohol."

Selah wasn't comforted by that fact. Her brother was going to work in the place he was terrified by last week. She continued to question what her brother was thinking, but then she remembered, he likely wasn't thinking at all. Her eyes pleaded with Tony to help her figure this mess out.

Selah sat back down next to Tony. She saw him wrestling with something in his mind. At this moment she wished she could read minds rather than glow like a night-light. He went to reach for her but instead got up and grabbed his jacket and helmet. "Let's stop stressing about something we can't quite make sense of till tomorrow night. How about we go for a sunset run on my bike?"

Selah got up and walked over to him. She stood for a moment looking up into his eyes. Before thinking twice, she wrapped her arms around his neck and held him tightly. She felt Tony slowly, tenderly bring his arm around her waist.

"Tony, thank you." She fit perfectly in the crook of his neck as she mumbled, "Thank you for watching out for my brother. I know you are doing it to help me, and it blesses me more than you could ever know." He squeezed her and took in a deep breath.

"Anytime, Say." His voice was husky and deep.

Selah let go first as she went to grab her faux leather jacket and slipped her shoes back on.

When they got to his bike, Tony helped Selah put on one of his helmets. He tucked a loose hair behind her ear, winked, then hopped on his bike. Selah did the same, straddling his beauty of a beast, electrified with excitement when she felt the bike roar to life. She instinctively wrapped her arms tight around Tony as he revved the engine. In the blink of an eye they shot off toward the pink, orange, and purple painted sky.

• CHAPTER 16 •

MICHAEL

Michael had witnessed a change in Selah at work this week. A part of him wished he could fix whatever was bothering her. He continually asked after Sean, hoping to give her a place to open up. Since the tragedy that took their father, Dean Moore, Officer Moore, his old partner, Michael had tried for weeks to ease the burden of their family's loss. During that time, he contemplated every way he could have prevented Dean's death. Michael wrestled with it often, even these years later. He understood that God would turn the heartache of Dean's children into good for them. But Michael, always the protector, wanted to curb their suffering. He accepted that his place was to help Selah in her purpose as one of the Chosen, but he hoped to help Selah and Sean both heal. The miracle of providence changed the pain and suffering that found its way into humanity. It made every situation meant to harm or destroy become a stepping stone for something spectacular. God would be sure to change the outcome for the Moore family and for all those who trusted in him.

The day Dean died, Michael grieved for the first time since the Crucifixion. He had become so ingrained in the Moore family's well-being that the pain felt by Elizabeth, Selah, and Sean felt like his own. Watching Sean these past few years destroy himself, and seeing the pain it had caused his family, made Michael feel helpless. A feeling he was not used to.

When Selah finally opened up and informed him that her brother was doing well, it came as a surprise. The last time they talked about Sean, he was numbing his pain continually in drugs and drinking. Michael had asked her what had changed, and as soon as she said the names of Marcus and Judas, he knew Sean was in more trouble than Selah could understand. These two were well-known lower demons dressed as humans, and had been taunting, terrorizing, and tempting the city for far too long. Their boss, Luc Vega, was Michael's brother, the Fallen One, Lucifer himself.

Michael hadn't been paying attention when Uriel asked him a question. Michael let the thought of his traitor brother fall away as Uriel cleared his throat to ask again. "So, should we go to the club tomorrow, Mikey?"

"Please refresh me as to why we would be going there? I am sorry, Brother, my mind was far away."

"Three of the Chosen will be there. Raphael used her influence to have Jaidyn ask Daniel to join them as back up. So...if the Chosen are all there shouldn't we be there too? To protect them, especially if Luc realizes they are there?"

Michael could hear the frustration in Uriel's last words, he understood how hard it must be for Uriel to work in disguise for the brother who had deeply betrayed them. They had suspected that Luc knew of Uriel's "other worldly" spirit but displayed no knowledge of knowing Uriel was his brother. In these human forms, each of them looked far different than their Heavenly bodies. Uriel, in his heavenly form would have six wings covered in eyes, a trait all of the seraphim shared. Unfortunately, that would just be a bit much for humans to grasp, so Uriel's disguise worked well. As frustrated as he was with being patient, he knew when to hold back, and when to fight. It helped too, that when Luc fell from Heaven, his ability to differentiate Heavenly bodies from human form was skewed. His only grace was to see the ugliness of the hell he created.

Michael finally answered, "Yes. I think that's a good idea." Then he looked at Gabriel; the Chosen knew him as Mr. Phillips, their math teacher at Freedom High. He was also the Archangel, one who once cared most deeply for Lucifer, and was deeply wounded by his betrayal. "Gabriel, I know this will not be easy for you, but it is time we finally step foot in Lucifer's domain. Are you ready?"

Gabriel's jaw tightened and his muscles twitched. "I knew this day was coming." He sighed. "It would be a relief to finally get it over with. I have thought about the day I would see him face-to-face again and what I would say, and I still have no idea. It just needs to happen. We need to see what he is planning and how deep his tentacles of power and deception are in this town." He paused, and shook his head. "Seeing Sean for myself and how he is getting stronger day by day is worrisome. That means the demon blood that is in the drug is mixing with his. We need to intervene and soon. We must also decide if now is the proper time to reveal ourselves to the Chosen. We need to begin their training. My vote is that we do it now."

Michael cringed at that thought. Gabriel the Messenger had spoken with power from up high, so his words had rung with truth. "Yes, I do believe you're right. I just talked about this with Raphael. Jaidyn and Selah are beginning to show signs of their abilities becoming stronger."

Gabriel added, "And Daniel is starting to show sure signs of God's promptings, understanding something is coming, but he doubts himself. I know he went to Selah yesterday worried about Sean. That, of course, was God, prompting them all to watch more closely. Daniel only doubted his deep concern when Selah said Sean was doing good. It's hard to watch them doubt when all we want to do is teach them that what they are feeling or doing is, in fact, real."

Uriel piped in, "Yeah, you're telling me, watching Tony as he protects Selah, ignites a motorcycle engine or lights up rooms by accident, not knowing what the heck is going on. There have been many times I have wanted to walk up to him and let him know he isn't crazy. And while he has been able to keep it under wraps for the most part, the day is coming soon for me to help him because his control is starting to wane."

"Then it sounds like it's time for us to step in, Michael," Raphael observed as she had been listening intently this whole time sipping her tea, surely contemplating every side of this decision.

"I agree," Michael said. "Tomorrow we watch them, observe their gifts, watch their investigation of AfterBurn, then from there we will decide when and how to reveal ourselves. I pray God guides us. This could get chaotic if we are not careful."

"Agreed," Uriel, Gabriel, and Raphael said in unison.

After that, their meeting relaxed. They sat and talked of work, mulling over how they would each teach their young cohorts. As exciting as it all was, Michael was burdened with the thought that if things went wrong, it could have a dire outcome.

• CHAPTER 17 •

SELAH

Selah found herself smiling every time last night's sunset ride with Tony replayed in her mind, though her nerves would won out when she thought about what they had planned for tonight. Although she was excited about going with Tony, the anxiousness of not knowing what they would see at AfterBurn grew by the moment. Her mind went back and forth over all the possibilities she could conceive while she cleaned her room.

She heard Sean come in late last night, and when she checked this morning he was still asleep in his room. Mom was in her pajamas, glued to some binge-worthy television show.

It donned on Selah that she forgot to tell her mom she'd made plans to go out tonight, and if her mom wasn't going anywhere Selah had no way of getting out of this house without asking her. She continued cleaning her room, next, the laundry, all of it a distraction from her constant running thoughts about tonight. She kept her expectations in check. But she knew she would have to ask her mom soon. *Maybe after this episode.*

Last night, Tony hadn't said anything to indicate he felt anything more than friendship for Selah, though at times when he looked into her eyes she swore she had seen some glimmer of longing. Had she given him a hint about her feelings? Come to think of it, she hadn't. She imagined herself with confidence enough to come right out and kiss him, while the realistic side of her brain crushed that daydream with the most likely outcome of her misjudging the timing and knocking heads with him or something just as stupendous.

She was driving herself crazy. She needed a human distraction. She called Jaidyn to come over.

Before Jaidyn could say her greeting, Selah blurted, "Hey, Jay, please come save me from my overthinking."

"Stressing over tonight, huh?" A smile warmed Jaidyn's voice. Selah was glad her best friend was getting some entertainment out of her self-made torture.

"Just hurry it up, and get over here!"

"Fine, Fine." She laughed. "I am on my way, Cinderella." Selah rolled her eyes. Jaidyn rattled on about feeling like Selah's fairy godmother getting her ready for the ball, then hung up. At least Cinderella didn't have hours to question herself before she went to the ball, because if she had, maybe she would have talked herself out of it. Selah lay back on her bed, stared up at the ceiling, and silently prayed.

God, please don't let me make a fool of myself tonight. And if there is something sinister going on at AfterBurn, please keep me from being so distracted that I don't notice.

Selah heard Jaidyn walk into the house. "Hi Aunt Beth." Jaidyn had called Selah's mom that since they were kids. Kathy, Jaidyn's mom had been close friends with Selah's mom since their college years.

"Hi, kiddo, what are you up to?"

"Just came by to help Selah get ready for tonight."

"Oh, what are you girls doing?"

Selah jumped off her bed and raced to the living room.

"Um, Mom, I kinda forgot to ask you if we could go out tonight. We will probably go see a movie and hang out afterward. I might be home late though, is that okay?"

Jaidyn looked at her with concealed amusement.

"Yeah, that's fine," she answered. Then she looked to Jaidyn. "What are you girls going to see?"

Before Jaidyn could ruin the story she was weaving, Selah piped up, "Either the new superhero movie or a tearjerker. Really depends on our mood, I guess." Selah was playing this off way too easily. She hoped to God it didn't backfire.

"Oh, okay. Well, have fun." She went back to watching her show as Selah turned to Jaidyn and signaled for their exodus.

Once they were in the room, Jaidyn closed the door and whispered, "Really Selah? Why lie about it? Your mom is cool. If it were my mom, we would be locked in my room all night with no hope of getting out."

"Well, then what did you tell your mom?"

Jaidyn raised her eyebrow suggesting Selah knew the answer already.

"You're right, my mom probably wouldn't care, but I just didn't want to explain that we were going to a club with Tony." Selah saw Jaidyn's face turn serious. "Why do you look like that?"

"Okay, Say, don't kill me." She paused. "I invited Daniel." Selah's jaw dropped as Jaidyn rattled on. "And I told my mom we were going to be studying here for a big test coming up. So…" She wore a don't-worry smile. "I am yours all night."

"Oh Jay, why did you invite Daniel? Not that he can't come, but I thought we had it covered with the three of us." *Not to mention the awkwardness of trying to tell Tony how I feel with my ex-boyfriend around.*

Selah made her mind up to wait for another time to tell Tony how she really felt. She had plenty of time to reveal that later. "Maybe Daniel's presence will help me focus on the real reason we are going tonight."

Jaidyn choked out a laugh. "How about we go get our nails done, my treat, since I kinda messed up your plans. I think when you finally tell Tony how you feel it won't be as hard as you think. I mean, he took you out last night on his motorcycle. When is the last time Tony let anyone other than himself even touch his 'baby'?" she said with exaggerated finger quotations, rolled eyes, and all.

It was Selah's turn to laugh. "Fine, fine. Let's go." Selah grabbed her purse. "I just wish my mind would calm down. I have literally thought of a hundred ways tonight will fail or be a total disaster. This day needs to be over already so I can breathe. I think once I see the doors of AfterBurn and Marcus's smug face my nerves will go out the window. Did you know Sean got a job there? And get this, so did Tony."

Jaidyn's jaw dropped. "Hold on, tell me everything on the way to the salon."

They made their way back out to the living room to the front door and said a quick goodbye to Selah's mom and let her know they would be right back. They jumped into Jaidyn's VW Bug. As she turned the key Selah continued her story.

After a moment Jaidyn chimed in. "So, wait, Tony is a bartender?" Jaidyn chuckled, "That's ironic."

Selah continued to explain what Tony had told her.

"Well that's noble of Tony. But what is Sean doing there?" Jaidyn's knuckles whitened as she tightened her grip on the steering wheel.

"He is apparently a part-time bouncer," Selah said.

Jaidyn let out a shaky breath, nodding her head as if it made sense. "Well, we likely would have seen him there anyway with how much he and Quinn are tied at the hip."

Selah heard the disgust in Jaidyn's tone. She couldn't blame her; she felt the same way.

CHAPTER 18

SELAH

Selah was motionless in the shower, the water slowly washing away the rest of her stress over tonight's anticipated adventure. As soon as she could feel her anxious thoughts ease she turned off the shower, hopped out, and walked back into her room where Jaidyn was getting ready. To Selah's relief, Jaidyn had come when she called, rescuing her from her anxious heart, though Selah had a sneaking suspicion that Jaidyn loved playing her fairy godmother.

"Wow, Jay, you look...amazing!" Jaidyn had on a sassy, black chiffon shirt with flowing bat-wing sleeves and skinny jeans paired with cute black suede booties. Her hair was partially clipped up with pheasant feathers and black leather strung with golden beads, which complemented her auburn hair. Jaidyn was a picture of boho chic crossed with indie rock sass.

"Thanks!" Jaidyn's smile warmed her face. "Time for you to get ready, Cinderella." She winked as she took Selah's outfit out of the closet. She handed it over to Selah, then escaped to the bathroom before Selah could say another word.

Selah quickly dressed, chancing a glance at her floor-length mirror, only to see the surprised look on her own face. Her outfit was all rock 'n' roll, complete with the black leather leggings, dark-purple waterfall neckline halter top that Jaidyn had picked out the other day, but it was the boots—they were her favorite—knee high and black leather. Whenever she wore them she felt powerful, like she was about to stomp on the devil himself. As she zipped the boots up, she heard her brother's voice in the hall. Selah instinctively grabbed her silver bangle bracelets and angel wing earrings, then followed his voice.

"What are you and my sis doing tonight?" Selah overheard him asking. "You look like you're gonna be up to no good." He grinned mischievously at Jaidyn, casually leaning on the doorjamb watching as she put on her makeup. When Selah reached the now shared doorway, she noticed the rosiness in Jaidyn's cheeks.

She jumped into their conversation to divert Sean's attention off poor Jaidyn. Selah lowered her voice to a whisper, "We are going out with Tony and Daniel." She decided to keep the fact that they were going to AfterBurn to herself. "We will likely see a movie or something." She berated herself for lying yet again, because it seemed it was quickly becoming second nature.

"Oh, Daniel and Tony, huh?" he teased. "Look at my big sis finally getting back in the game." He gave her a conspiring grin. Before she could stop herself, Selah punched him in the arm.

"Do shut up, will you? Mom doesn't know we are going with them. I kinda left that part out." She sighed. "I don't know why she is always more concerned about my love life than yours."

Sean laughed. "Maybe because she gave up on me having a real relationship a year ago. I did kinda date half the girls at our school." Yeah, she didn't need reminding of her brother's casual liaisons. Jaidyn coughed like she was choking. Selah looked at her, confused.

"You okay, Jay?" She rubbed Jaidyn's back to soothe her. Jaidyn stepped to the side so they could share the mirror. Selah looked back at her brother, annoyed at how well he looked. She was certain something was amiss with him. "Privacy please!" She nodded her head toward the hall guiding him to go away.

"Fine." He began to leave, then turned around. "Hey, I will be home a little late tonight, but don't worry about me I will be waiting for Quinn to get off work."

Selah rolled her eyes as he left and closed the door behind him.

Jaidyn let out a huge sigh of relief.

"You okay?" Selah asked. Jaidyn seemed shaken by her brother's interrogation.

"Yeah, I am fine. Though I am still worried about Sean. I can't put my finger on it, but he feels off. Even with the last few years of drama he still was Sean, but now when he is around I feel a deep emptiness." She shook her head. "I probably sound crazy."

Selah answered while applying her mascara. "No, not at all. I was felt the same thing. Something is just off. I can't pin it down either. Except, of course, that he's dating Quinn. That's just a whole other level of weird."

Jaidyn blanched and dropped her lip gloss. She recovered quickly. They finished up quickly since Daniel and Tony were meeting them at the club in a half hour.

Selah walked into the living room. Her mom had gone to her own room for something. Selah instantly grabbed her cropped black leather jacket, nearly catching it on one of the zippers on her purse. She yelled down the hall, "Bye, Mom, we will be back later tonight!" She hurried out the door before her mom could come out. She had no time for explanations nor was she sure she could keep up the charade if her mom asked for any more details.

"Bye girls, have fun!" Mom didn't budge, thank God.

Maybe it was false confidence, but Selah finally felt like she was ready. Ready to find out what After-Burn was all about and to go to a club for the first time in her existence. She no longer cared that she might be walking into danger; as long as she had Jaidyn with her they could conquer tonight's mission. She looked forward to letting loose. A part of her spirit really needed that. But gathering proof of AfterBurn's dark side balanced the wildness that was rising up inside of her. She smiled at Jaidyn over the top of her purple VW Bug. "You ready to go have some fun?"

With a devilish smirk she replied, "Oh, they're not ready for us!"

CHAPTER 19

MICHAEL

After more than a millennium fighting evil as an Archangel, Michael could feel the unease of facing Lucifer sitting in his stomach, like a lead weight. He had watched from afar the comings and goings of AfterBurn, but tonight they would be entering Luc's territory while in human form. While each of the Archangels would be unrecognizable, that fact didn't ease Michael's mind. He had sat back and watched Lucifer's greed, lust, and evil influence each person that came into his club. Michael and the Angels had to wait for that pivotal moment when they could finally confront Lucifer.

Since the moment the Archangels stepped foot on Earth in human flesh, Michael understood there would be no more of the old way of doing things. No mountain-shattering fights to the death or battles in the spiritual realm that would quake the world. Many times, humans would witness these battles as lightning cracking across a stormy sky, small earthquakes rattling the earth, or violent winds ripping up trees from the root. Each battle Michael fought resulted in Lucifer and his followers, the Fallen, being sent back to Hell. Rarely did Lucifer leave the protection of his realm, or fight his own battles for that matter. It made their plan that much more important—everything done in its proper time.

Michael had the gifts of strength and strategy, whereas Lucifer had always been diabolical and cunning. When Luc conjured up a way to walk on Earth as a human, God decided to send his finest warriors to do the same. The inevitable confrontation would have to be done in a way that kept humans from seeing the Angels' supernatural bodies and abilities. They would have no way to change to their Angelic forms without raising some eyebrows. For the last two decades they have been playing Luc Vega's cat and mouse game; now that the Chosen were growing into their abilities, the time was near for Lucifer to be sent back to Hell.

Michael worked on clearing his mind with each step he took toward Raphael's apartment. Sadly, it was only a short distance, too short to get the peace he desired. Michael stood at the door and knocked.

"You ready?" he called through the door. He saw Gabriel and Uriel walking down the adjoined hall of their apartment complex.

"Hey, Mikey, I'm gonna take Lucille. I will meet you all there." Why Uriel named his motorcycle such a ridiculous name, Michael had no idea.

"Sure, see ya there." He turned back to the door as Uriel headed to the parking lot. "Raph, come on, we are trying to get there before they close tonight."

Gabriel laughed next to Michael as he leaned against the wall. "Why is it Raphael is one of the toughest warriors I know, yet she can't help herself from getting dolled up like a true human female?" The irony was she did not need any of it. Just as Gabriel finished his question, Raphael opened her door. Both Gabriel and Michael's jaws dropped as she filled the hall with light.

"Um, Raph!" Michael shot an amused look up at her. She was incredible in her Angelic form—tall, intimidating, and full of healing light. He raised his eyebrow with a hinting stare, then glanced from side to side to make sure no one else was in the hall. "You better slip back into human form before we leave."

Gabriel shook his head. "Geez! Is that what was taking you so long?"

"Sorry, I just needed to stretch these babies out." She smirked and shook her wings out, then a bright shimmering light swirled around her and she was changed back to her human self. She did it so quickly, anyone who blinked would have missed it. She stepped out into the hallway, shut her door, and locked it. She took both her brothers by their elbows and grinned at them. "Sorry about that. Now...let's go make a lasting impression on our proteges, shall we?"

It always amazed Michael how different each of their human forms was, especially being forebears from the same Creator, they looked completely different from each other. The only common factor was their continual low hum of golden aura. It was similar to the glow each of their proteges was gifted, the Mark of Heaven.

Michael looked at his siblings and imagined how well they would blend in at this club of Luc's. Raph had fair skin, blond hair, dangerously long legs, and celestial blue eyes—all a stunning, stark glimpse of Heaven's light. Any human male would likely fall over himself to talk to her.

Gabriel's skin was a light golden tan, and he had almond-shaped titanium-gray eyes, a slim nose and warm smile; while he stood at an average height he had the lean muscular build of a highly trained martial arts master. Gabriel, had a gentle, commanding presence, and would do fine blending in tonight. The one who seemed far better at blending in than all of them was Uriel, with his tattoos, piercings, and muscles. The only thing that separated him from his siblings was the inch-long severe scar over his right eyebrow, a souvenir of his battle with Abaddon and the demon sword he wielded, forged with Lucifer's own blood. The scar that no matter how much Raph tried would not completely heal. It was a flaw that gave Uriel a much more mortal appearance than the rest of them, making his job as AfterBurn's bouncer that much more believable.

Raphael pulled into the club's parking lot. Michael listened as Gabriel and Raphael made guesses as to which of the Chosen would react the most shocked when the Angels revealed themselves. Both agreed it would be Selah. Michael thought for sure it would be Daniel. They would find out soon enough.

Raphael parked. As they got out of the car and began walking to the front of the club the nervous energy between them all was palpable.

Raphael was dressed to the nines in a body-contouring dress the color of dried lavender, and glittering silver heels. Gabriel was dressed in a light-gray dress shirt, tailored dark-gray pants, and a dark shimmering gray dress jacket. Michael was the picture of casual sophistication with black slacks and a white long-sleeve dress shirt rolled up to his elbows and the top two buttons unbuttoned. They looked like they belonged here, thanks to Raph's fashion research. When they reached the entrance, he nodded at Uriel and got in line.

Michael scanned the parking lot for Selah and the other Chosen. Raphael was fixing her lip gloss, and Gabriel was striking up conversation with fellow clubgoers in line. Raph looked up and said, "They're here." She looked past her brothers toward the parking lot just as Tony came roaring into the parking lot on his motorcycle.

CHAPTER 20

TONY

Tony spotted Selah as he scanned the parking lot. He couldn't help but watch her from this distance. He might be all about sobriety, but there was something deeply hypnotic about the way Selah carried herself. Tony collected his wayward thoughts, then dismounted his all-black custom Harley, and left his helmet on the handle bar. He glanced back to Selah and caught sight of Jaidyn and Daniel. *What is Daniel doing here?* He didn't realize Daniel was coming; he had just talked to him on Wednesday, and he didn't say anything about coming tonight.

"Hey Daniel." Tony clapped him on the back as he walked up behind him, giving his shoulder a friendly squeeze. Daniel wore fitted jeans and black button up dress shirt and red tie with his hair slicked back, not even one hair out of place. Daniel's look wasn't much different from Tony's. Tony donned a white dress shirt with a thin black tie, and his unmistakable, every day black leather jacket. He'd actually made an attempt at styling his hair—his undercut faux hawk stood at attention. Tony gave a dazzling smile to Selah and Jaidyn, then back to Daniel. "I am surprised to see you at this fine establishment."

Tony had known Daniel long enough to know that he would rather chill and play video games or hang with his football friends than be here. Tony would bet money on that fact. Then he saw the way he was looking at Selah.

Selah anxiously caught Tony's eyes as he gave Daniel a friendly side hug. He knew Daniel and Selah had history, though he really didn't care. Daniel had had his chance, and Tony was not afraid of competition. He laughed to himself, when he saw Selah sweating it out.

He turned his attention to Jaidyn. "Hey, Jay, looking good, lady." He took her hand and twirled her around, smiled at her, and put his arm around her neck and pulled her into a brotherly hug. He glanced over Jaidyn's head, and caught Selah watching them. He could see a hint of sadness in her eyes.

Letting go of Jaidyn, Tony walked over and stopped right in front of Selah, her eyes that dizzying blue-green that always enchanted him. "Selah," he said her name with a low growl and grinned. "You certainly pulled out all the stops tonight. He stepped back to check her out properly; his eyes roved over her from her eyes to her boots, and back, only to see the blush that rushed to her cheeks. *That's better.* He got closer and slid his arm around her waist and pulled her into a deep hug, drawing in her sweet honey-lemon scent. *God above help me.* Deep down he knew the way he felt about Selah was dangerous. He slowly pulled away. "Them boots are official buttkicking boots." He laughed. "No one can say you don't come prepared." He quirked a devilish sideways smile, and her eyes sparkled as she smiled back. He broke the tension inside him and turned to include Daniel and Jaidyn. "Ready?"

"Ready as I will ever be," Jaidyn said as she winked at Selah who was trying to gather her wits about her. She took Selah's arm, and they marched toward the club.

Daniel hung back, nervously opening and shutting his mouth.

"What's up?" Tony curiously asked.

"Okay, Tone, I'm just gonna ask. Do you like Selah? Because lately you have been laying it on a bit thick."

Tony's eyebrow shot up in question, then he sucked on his teeth in thought.

"Daniel, the fact you have to ask that tells me I haven't laid it on thick enough." He guffawed. "I respect her far more than you know, and I hope to win her over, but I don't see that happening with everything going on with Sean right now. But if I can make her feel anything other than worry, anger, or pain, I think she deserves it."

Daniel actually looked taken aback. "Wow, I guess I never saw it before. I didn't know you had feelings for her. Weren't you recently dating Anne-Marie?"

At the mention of her name Tony cringed. He hadn't mentioned this to Selah yesterday, because it was over as soon as it started. Nothing happened, Anne-Marie was poison from the start.

"I mean I know she was a piece of work, but I beg you, Tone, don't hurt Selah. She and I may never be together again, but I do care about her." With that heartfelt proclamation the conversation ended, and they stepped in line.

Selah turned to them. "What are you two talking about?" Her questioning gaze made Tony squirm. What would happen if she found out about him and Anne-Marie? The story he'd told her yesterday was the truth. While that story wasn't his, it scared him enough to keep his guard up. Tony knew ugly truths about Anne-Marie and Quinn. Truths most people would think were crazy, but he had seen that evil with his own eyes.

"Just about how great you ladies look tonight." He gave a playful wink. If he could figure out a way to tell Selah now, he would. Instead, he promised himself when the right time came he would tell her. He knew it wouldn't be easy to break that truth. Anne-Marie and Quinn had been horribly abusive to Selah for so long that knowing he had once dated her childhood nemesis could very well make her run the other direction. He pushed that far from his mind as the girls tried to move toward the end of the line.

They had seen their bosses and Mr. Phillips, their math teacher in line and wanted to stay hidden.

When they finally reached the door, they gave their identification. Tony's favorite bouncer was back at it again. "Sunshine" feigned a smile at all of them as he checked their IDs and waved them in. The place was flooded with pulsing lights and thumping music, and like a wave it hit them as they entered.

Selah shouted over the music, "Let's get a booth so we can watch what's going on." She maneuvered her way through the crowd to the same back corner Tony had picked on his first visit. *Great minds.*

Tony's eyes danced around the club as he followed Selah. He could see people he knew grinding and swaying to the beat. In the VIP section closest to the DJ booth, he spotted Sean, Marcus, and Judas, each of them slinging back drinks. His steps faltered when he saw Anne-Marie. *Speak of the devil.* He witnessed as she marched straight over to Judas and smacked him. Judas in shock, grabbed her arm, and in one fierce motion pulled her down and began kissing her, hard. *Wow!* He hadn't expected that. He turned away from that wreckage and finished making his way toward the booth where Selah and the others waited.

CHAPTER 21

MICHAEL

Once inside the club, Michael took a moment to scan the crowd as Raphael walked over to the closest open booth. It was in the perfect spot for people watching. Michael sat down and could see every angle of the club, even with all the moving bodies, lights, and simulated fog. The club had just opened and was already packed from wall to wall.

Leave it to the once legendary Angel of Worship to draw a crowd of hedonistic partygoers.

Michael's attention was drawn to the back of the club, to a curtained-off booth where Selah and Jaidyn were sitting. He watched Daniel head to the bar and grab drinks. Tony entered Michael's line of sight; he was stock-still in the middle of the dance floor. Michael traced Tony's line of sight, and saw Judas, one of Luc's lackeys, kissing a succubus. Michael was certain that Tony was unable to see what he saw, at least not yet anyway. Michael studied the succubus. She had glittering green skin, with scales like a snake and the eyes to match.

Michael's eyebrows knit together in concentration, hoping Tony wasn't under her spell. Michael didn't know this succubus, but from now on, he would keep an eye out for her. Michael was relieved when Tony finally turned away and walked over to Selah's booth.

Michael relaxed. He sat back, casually placing his arm on the booth next to his sister, his eyes not resting while he continued to scan the room. He had a hard time letting his guard down, especially knowing Luc Vega was hiding somewhere in the shadows, probably watching his brood of vipers while they influenced young unsuspecting victims.

Michael witnessed as humans danced with hellhounds, lower-demons, incubi, and succubi, bodies intertwined, full of desire and mischief. There were Earthly myths referring to each of these types of demons. In Heaven they were only known as The Fallen—fallen angels who fed on human souls, flesh, and blood. The lust of these demons drove them to procreate with human women, which bore the Nephilim. The Fallen thought they could outsmart God, creating new monsters of their own. Soon after they endured the wrath of God. Lucifer and his Fallen were warned that if they mated with humans ever again they would be sent to the Abyss and would never even see Hell again. To Michael's knowledge, none of them had tried since.

It still made Michael sick that Luc was able to prance among the humans. For too long he watched him and the Fallen toy with humanity. All these monsters ever did was pervert truth, leading humans to destruction. Michael grew more and more tired of their antics.

He was grateful though, that it wasn't only the Archangels that kept these demons in line. Cherubim, their comrades, were Angels that could change from human form to any animal they needed to utilize, and by doing so they were able to infiltrate areas that the Archangels could not. There were also the seraphim, Angels usually only found in their spiritual form, who presided over every continent of Earth like gatekeepers. Some continents had more than one Seraphim Guard based on the number of human souls they watched over. Seraphim were the Guarding Light of Heaven, they kept demons from entering Heaven and helped guide the human race toward Heaven when they passed on from this world to the next.

Uriel, as it happened, was one of those seraphim; although, after the Fall of Man, Uriel's righteous anger fueled him to join the Archangels. His hope was to keep Lucifer's influence on this world to a minimum. Uriel was, in fact, the very seraphim that had escorted Adam and Eve out of Eden. Since that day, humanity's protection had been his number one drive, as well as the other Archangels'. The human race was completely unaware of all these things; they had no idea what the Angels had done and continued to do, to protect them.

Gabriel came back with his hands full of drinks, breaking Michael's train of thought. He handed a club soda to Michael. Raphael got the closest thing they had to a strawberry milkshake, a virgin strawberry daiquiri.

"Thanks Gabe." Michael took a sip while Gabriel sat down. "What do you think of the succubus that is hanging on Judas? Have any of you seen her before?"

Both of them turned at the same time, looking around. They finally saw her.

Gabriel looked disgusted. "Yeah, I have seen her at Freedom High. I don't have her in my class, but her name is Anne-Marie," he said with distaste. "She has manipulated a handful of young men. I was able to keep a close eye on each of them, and luckily none of them were close to the Death Walk. I was able to talk some sense into each of them. I have to admit though I am glad to see her messing with a fellow demon rather than any of my students."

"She worries me; from what I witnessed earlier I think Tony may know her. I don't think she has any influence over him, but I'd rather be cautious anyway. We definitely don't need any of the Chosen doing a Death Walk."

The Death Walk was the slow, dead-eyed march, one only a man fully committed to take his life or the life of someone else, all for his lover. There was little that could break the influence of a succubus's power once the Death Walk set in.

"Agreed," both Gabe and Raphael said in unison. They continued to watch the mixed crowd from their vantage point. They watched Daniel walk Jaidyn out to the dance floor.

Michael glimpsed at Raphael as she watched Jaidyn. She was following Jaidyn's line of sight, then let out a sigh. Jaidyn's tear-filled eyes were on Sean, who was preoccupied with the succubus dancing in his lap. Daniel looked down at Jaidyn's face and saw her expression change from disgust to sheer pain. Michael observed the pain on Raph's face too. In that moment, Daniel began dancing like a fool. Jaidyn's laugh brought a smile back to Raph's face and lightened Michael's heart too.

"Daniel is a good guy," she said out loud.

Gabriel was Daniel's guardian and protector. He smiled and watched the dance floor as Daniel continued to dance like an imbecile. Gabriel shook his head. "Yeah, he sure is something."

CHAPTER 22

SELAH

When Jaidyn and Daniel hit the dance floor, Selah's nerves began firing at a rapid pace. They had left her alone with Tony. *When did I start feeling nervous around Tony?* He was always so easygoing, funny, and kind. It was Jaidyn's fault; she was the one who pointed out that Tony liked her as more than a friend. Now Selah felt like a fangirl, one part of her dying to talk to him, the other wanting to hide under a rock.

She took a steadying breath and glanced quickly at him to see if he was looking at her. She noticed his faraway stare. He was watching the booth Sean, Marcus, and Judas were sprawled out in. They looked like they owned the VIP section.

Quinn was all over her brother, making the bile rise up into her throat. But it wasn't them Tony was staring at, it was the whispering and giggling Anne-Marie that had his attention. He watched as she rubbed Judas's thigh. *What is he thinking?* Selah faked a coughed. Tony turned his attention back to her.

Selah asked, "What are you looking at?"

He looked like he was about to be sick himself. He shook his head.

Selah wasn't sure if it was shame or to shake Anne-Marie from his mind. The look on his face was disappointment. "I was watching Anne-Marie. She makes my skin crawl."

"Yeah, you aren't the only one," Selah said, hoping he really meant it.

"Say." He turned his full attention on her. "I need to tell ya something. I really hope it doesn't change how you see me."

She raised a brow with intrigue.

"Okay…"

He looked like he had done something unforgivable before he confessed. "I dated Anne-Marie last year," he blurted. "Well if you can even call it that really. We were together for a week before I started having these strange anxiety attacks."

Selah's eyes softened into a smile. Then he did mean what he said earlier.

He continued. "I realized it had to be Anne-Marie since it would happen every time I was around her. That's when I decided to break it off."

Selah looked down at her hands, trying to keep the relief from showing on her face. She hated Anne-Marie, but she didn't want Tony to feel any worse than he already did.

"I had talked with one of her exes, remember that one guy I told ya about? Well, I counted myself lucky that she didn't do to me what she had done to him. But even now when I see her, I feel like she is about to ruin my whole life in one fell swoop." He took a deep breath. He caught Selah's eyes, his full of intent. "I know it sounds crazy, but I really had to get that off my chest."

Selah quirked a carefree smile. "I already knew."

He looked shocked.

"I saw you guys out together once driving in her car. I knew something was up, but the next time I saw you she wasn't around, and hasn't been since, so

I figured whatever had been going on was over." She patted his hand in comfort. "Just glad you came out in one piece." Her shoulders relaxed, and her anxiousness fell away.

He beamed and grabbed her hand before she could pull it away. He was looking at her like that again, like he was wrestling with a confession. "I thought about you often, even then—that's probably what saved me. I always thought about how horrible Anne-Marie had been to you, well, to everyone. I wasn't even sure how or why I was considering a relationship with her. I think she would have eaten my heart." He kept his eyes locked on Selah's, a playful grin on his lips, as he caressed her hand with his thumb.

She blushed. Selah was sure she was camouflaged with the red vinyl on the booth. His grin only intensified into that sunshine smile he shared so rarely, making her smile reflect his own.

"You thought about me?" She flirtatiously raised her eyebrow in question. He laced his fingers into hers. He moved in closer to her and whispered loudly enough to be heard over the house music, "It was all kind, believe me. Anne-Marie is so not you. It was like she was a dark endless tunnel and you were my guiding light."

She gawked at him, questioning his sanity as he went on.

"I don't think you understand how you touch the world around you. Since the day Mom and Dad died, you and my grandma have been my constants. If I could give you that back by helping you with Sean, I would do it a thousand times. I promise to do all I can to give you that same comfort, of knowing you're not alone." He backed away to see her face. "I am at your service." His words made her deliciously lightheaded.

"Thank you, Tony." She tried desperately to keep from blushing more. "That is like the nicest thing anyone has said to me, especially when it comes to Sean. I am blessed to have friends like you and Jaidyn." She hoped *friends* didn't imply her disinterest, but she really didn't know what else to say. She caught herself glancing at his mouth and bit her lip. If he only knew how hard it had been to watch him that day when he got out of the car and kissed Anne-Marie. Selah swore she would give up anything for his kiss.

He leaned in again. "I am always here for you."

He surprised her then as he quickly got out of the booth. He shucked off his leather jacket, revealing his tight toned physique under his closely fitted dress shirt.

Don't lose your cool. She took a deep breath.

Tony held out his hand. "Let's go dance."

Jaidyn and Daniel walked up to the booth as they were leaving. Tony asked Jaidyn, "Hey, can you watch my jacket?" with his award-winning smile shining again, twice in one night.

He guided Selah toward the dance floor as Jaidyn called back, "Sure." Then she climbed into the booth. Daniel sat across from her.

Tony was walking behind her now, his hands on her hips trying to hold tight so as not to lose her to the bevy of writhing bodies. They had reached the middle of the dance floor when Tony turned her around and began swaying them both to the beat of the music. Selah could feel eyes on her but didn't dare see who was watching. She was trying to concentrate on her breathing as she rocked in sync with Tony. She glanced up at him when she noticed her skin was blazing with its warm glow.

Tony marveled at her and moved in closer. His lip grazed her ear as he breathed, "Your glow is breathtaking." His words soothed her, she was floating in his embrace. Part of her wanted to hide. She looked down at her feet hoping to keep herself from tripping over his. No one had ever said a kind thing about her glow, ever, except of course her dad before he passed, her mom, and Jaidyn, but they were a bit biased. She tilted her head back to see his face. Sure enough, she saw the truth in his eyes. She lost control of her senses as she reached up to touch his smooth face, her hand slipped around his neck. Before a second thought could cross her mind, *she kissed him*. It was a kiss filled with the warmth of her glow. She felt him lean into her, and her heart raced.

Tony broke the kiss, looking down at her stunned.

Oh God, I shouldn't have done that.

She tried to stand on her own two feet with confidence, but it slowly slipped away when Tony smiled.

"Finally," he said.

A scuffle near the bar caught their attention. Both of them turned their heads, along with everyone else on the dance floor, and in a heartbeat of a moment, a gunshot rang through the club.

MICHAEL

From Michael's line of sight, he saw a broad, dark man stalking to the bar. That stalking stride was a familiar one—Baleel, one of Luc's greater demon pawns. Baleel leaned on the bar talking to one of the bartenders. He glanced over at Daniel, who was getting Jaidyn another drink. Baleel said something to Daniel that Michael couldn't hear. Even with his advanced hearing, the club music was overpowering.

Daniel turned toward Baleel.

Michael's nerves sparked with anticipation, his senses on high alert. A glint of light gleamed from Baleel's hand that was hidden under the bar top.

Michael sprung to his feet.

Before Michael could reach them, Baleel shrugged at Daniel and pulled the trigger.

Daniel's eyes filled with shock as he dropped to the floor.

The music and dancing ceased.

Mayhem ensued.

Uriel and his bouncers pushed through the scrambling crowd and were instantly on top of Baleel.

Raphael and Gabriel followed Michael to Daniel, fighting the flow of people frantically heading for the front and back doors.

"Michael, we need to find them." He knew what Raphael meant and began to scan the crazy chaotic crowd, people continued to scramble as if the gunman was still firing on them.

Uriel nodded to Gabriel to let him know that he had Baleel, allowing them to continued looking for the rest of the Chosen.

"By the back door." Gabriel, kneeling by Daniel, nodded toward the back door at Michael as Jaidyn, Tony, and Selah were trying to exit.

Quickly, the Angels moved, and within seconds, they were next to them. Michael gently grabbed Selah's elbow. "Selah, you guys come with us." Jaidyn and Tony recognized him as Officer Shields. Without a second thought they followed Michael to the side entrance of the club.

He looked back to Uriel to make sure he was indeed okay to handle Baleel. Michael spotted Luc Vega. He stood next to Uriel talking with the other bouncers. Michael could hear him as he told them to leave for the night and close up the club. Raphael walked over to Michael. She had tried to administer healing to Daniel, but by the look on her face he could tell it had been too late. Michael put his arm around her neck and hugged her. "Take them to the safe house. I will stay with Gabriel and Uriel. We will meet you there."

She nodded in understanding and left the club behind.

Michael met Gabriel's golden tear-filled eyes, then looked to Uriel. "Why don't you both meet up with Raph and the others at the safe house? I can meet up with you after the police arrive. I will make sure Daniel's body is safe." Michael hung his head in shame. This shouldn't have happened. Not on their watch. Michael knew the Gailton Police Department would come soon; he also knew that there was no arresting Baleel. Luc was likely about to dispense of Baleel and tell the officers his own version of the story.

Michael's only concern was that Daniel's body was safe from Luc or any of his cohorts. Demons were known to do unsavory things to the dead. If he couldn't keep him safe in life, he wouldn't let him down in death. Gabriel would feel this loss far more deeply as Daniel's guardian—even Angels had a hard time dealing with loss.

Gabriel choked on his sobs. "Let me stay, Brother."

Uriel looked at Michael. Then with compassion he grasped Gabriel's shoulder. "Come on Gabe, let's go."

"I really should be the one to make sure he is taken care of." Another golden tear fell down his cheek.

"You had no idea this would happen, none of us did. I will make sure he is safe and we must prepare the others. This *will* not happen again. It is my fault, we should have done so sooner." Michael continued as Uriel went to grab his motorcycle jacket from the back of the bar. "I will meet you at the safe house. There is much work ahead of us."

Gabriel pursed his lips and gave a regretful nod.

Michael watched them leave through the front door, then looked down at Daniel's lifeless body, the blood around him pooling, a bullet hole through his heart. Michael rubbed the back of his neck as he heard the sirens blaring down the street.

By this time, many of the club's occupants had left to go home. Some were dispersed throughout the parking lot talking to the police. Gabriel and Uriel decided to wait also. Gabriel asked, "This must have been the first time something like this has happened. I don't ever remember you mentioning gunfights at the club."

Uriel shook his head, looking stoic, arms crossed as he leaned against his motorcycle.

"Definitely the first. Not that there haven't been other issues here. Judas did rip out an incubus's heart a couple weeks ago. Though, I wasn't on duty when it happened. The violence here is starting to become deadlier, especially for the humans. Michael's right, we should have warned the Chosen; they need to be trained, and the sooner the better."

Gabriel nodded. He couldn't understand why a demon would shoot Daniel, especially in the middle of a public place. Gabriel also knew that Luc would find some way to cover his tracks, likely by concocting some crazy story to keep the police scrutiny to a minimum.

He watched as the siren lights continued to flash around in the parking lot. He spotted Luc, now without his dress jacket, covered with ash. He was dusting himself off when the cops met him at the front entrance. He either influenced their minds or came up with a great story because they didn't even walk into the club. Gabriel knew that the ash on Luc was the remnants of Baleel, who was now back in Hell, hopefully to stay.

The only official to walk in or out of the club was the coroner, who came out with Daniel's body on a gurney covered by a sheet, blood seeping through at the chest. Gabe watched Michael follow the coroner. All the police officers climbed back into their cars and left, along with all the witnesses. Uriel began to put on his helmet.

Gabriel mumbled, "I will need to ride with you Uri."

"Climb on then." He got behind Uriel, no helmet, which didn't matter much; they could use their spiritual glamour and no one would even see them pass by.

The safe house was an old run-down church, complete with stained glass windows and a steeple. It was the church that Daniel's grandfather once pastored till they moved to a different location. The Angels had retrofitted it to work as a safe house and training facility. They trained here often, working on maneuvers to help maintain their Angel strength and abilities. They even set up a small housing area in the back, in anticipation for when the Chosen would be ready to train. The building was protected by Heaven and was a sanctuary of sorts, where the Chosen could learn from their guardians, train, and find rest. Uriel and Gabriel pulled up to the church and saw Raph's and the others' vehicles lined up outside. Gabriel prepared himself for the onslaught of questions, unsure if Raph had told them that Daniel was gone.

• CHAPTER 24 •

SELAH

One moment her lips were tingling from the kiss with Tony, the next a scream of horror had escaping. Her head was still trying to get a grip on reality.

She remembered Tony grabbing her, motioning at Jaidyn to come with them out the back door. She remembered seeing her brother's shocked face when he recognized her, but he quickly left with Quinn out the back door before she ever reached him. Then Raphael, Jaidyn's boss, guided them out the side door. Jaidyn was white with shock and still hadn't said a word. They were apparently headed to a safe house on the other side of Gailton. Selah couldn't figure out what *they* needed to be *safe* from.

She and Jaidyn had followed Raphael in Jaidyn's car. As they pulled into the parking lot of Daniel's grandfather's old church, Selah gave a questioning glance to Jaidyn, but she obviously was still in shock. Her knuckles were as white as her face with the tight grip she had on the steering wheel. Selah heard Tony roar in behind them on his motorcycle. She watched, waiting for Daniel to pull in next. Maybe he stayed behind with Officer Shields to give a witness statement.

As they got out of their cars, Uriel, the bouncer, and Mr. Phillips pulled up. Once off the motorcycle, Mr. Phillips silently led the way to the entrance of the old church. All the scary movies she and Jaidyn had watched with her mom were coming to mind. Selah swallowed down her fear and asked, "What exactly are we doing here?"

"Come in, then we can tell you more," Raphael assured. "I know this seems strange; believe me when I say it will not be the strangest thing you hear tonight."

Jaidyn linked her arm in Selah's as they all walked in. Mr. Phillips hit a few light switches, and all around them the gutted-out church was lit up. There was a large gym mat in the middle of the church. On the left side of the mat there was equipment for sparring and various sizes of boxing gloves hanging from a rack on the wall. In the corner were two life-size boxing dummies and a rack of staffs and wooden swords. *Is this some kind of martial arts studio?*

Selah craned her neck to take in the expanse of tall ceilings, gothic architecture, and the colorful windows with depictions of Jesus, well-known stories from the Bible, and Angels. If she had to guess, she figured the ceilings were fifty feet tall, and the windows felt nearly as large.

Mr. Phillips guided the way to a walled-off room at the back of the church, which included a couple couches, a TV, and a refrigerator, surrounded by an array of bookshelves packed full with books on every subject. The room itself probably took up a third of the building. A staircase to the side of the room led to a loft upstairs.

This place was enormous.

Selah looked at Jaidyn and Tony; they too were trying to take this all in.

"Is this some sort of gym?" Tony asked.

"You could say that," said a voice from behind them near the front door. Officer Shields walked in. Selah took a breath, waiting again to see Daniel. *Where is he?* Her worry now skated toward paranoia.

"Kind of, but I will get to that later." His face was full of gloom. "Let's all sit first."

Selah's heart dropped, something was wrong.

"Okay, can someone please tell us what is going on? We heard someone got shot, and you bring us to a gym? That doesn't seem like protocol whatsoever." She crossed her arms over her chest, imploring Officer Shields to cough it up.

"I know. First I need to tell you that Daniel was the one shot."

Selah's face blanched, confusion gripped her mind, but he went on.

"This should have never happened. For the first time in my long life, I am unsure where to start. But maybe the truth is the best place. As you know my name is Michael, this is my sister Raphael, and my brothers Uriel and Gabriel, and we are Angels."

Daniel would have made a remark how they must have been crazy. Selah's eyes flooded with tears, and her mind reeled. *Am I dreaming?*

"We were sent here for the same purpose. What you see in front of you are not our true forms."

Jaidyn sat down and changed the subject back to Daniel. "I saw that guy shoot Daniel." She began to sob. Selah sat next to her and wrapped her up in her arms.

"Why would that man want to hurt Daniel?" She wavered between anger and sadness, totally perplexed over how this could have happened. Tony stood next to them with his arms over his chest, deep in thought.

"It is a long story, but the man that shot him was not human; he must have known Daniel was one of you, one of the Chosen. At least, that is what I can gather at the moment." At Michael's statement the three of them looked at him like he was crazy.

Tony questioned, "One of us? The Chosen? What does that even mean?"

"The man was not human?" Jaidyn remarked right after Tony.

Raphael held Jaidyn's hand. "Each of you, Daniel included, have been hand-picked by God to defend your families and your city. Michael, Uriel, Gabe, and myself were given the privilege to bless you with abilities to help you in this purpose. We have been here on Earth since right before you were born." She sighed. "And tonight, we were too late to save Daniel, but we hope to help you guys before the Fallen come after you."

"Let me go back a little bit," Michael added. "You have known each of us in different parts of your lives. Gabriel has been the Freedom High math teacher. He was also your middle school math teacher; not sure you remember that."

Jaidyn and Selah nodded. They had known Mr. Phillips for a long time.

"Raphael has been the Gailton town vet for over fifteen years, and now your boss." He nodded toward Jaidyn, then looked to Selah. "I was your dad's partner on the force and a friend of your family."

Selah grimaced, clamping down on the frustration and pain burning in her heart. How could she lose her dad and now Daniel, and yet be surrounded by Angels?

Michael finished, "Uriel." He pointed to Uriel who was leaning against the table with the same stance as Tony. "He has been the bouncer for AfterBurn since it opened, even worked as security guard for a while at your grandparents' mobile home park, Tony. Each of us was given the specific task of watching after you until your abilities became more apparent. That is why we had to wait. Before now you would have been unable to fight the Fallen and succeed."

Jaidyn, Selah, and Tony looked at one another with uncertainty. Selah hadn't shared the growing instincts inside of her, the gifts she couldn't explain. When she looked at her friends now, she could see they had been dealing with the same struggle.

"I know you haven't even told each other about your abilities, and yes, for the Chosen they are normal, especially as you grow closer to adulthood."

Selah looked at her hands, her emotions making it hard to hide the glow again.

"Selah, this is why you have this glow. In fact, if you take a scrutinizing look at your friends you will see that you are not the only one." She blushed but concentrated on Tony and Jaidyn's form not an everyday glance, but a real hard look at each of them.

"And, Tony, you have had the uncanny ability to set things ablaze with a fire that burns deep within your bones," Michael divulged. "You also protect those you love and can quickly fix broken things. Uriel has tried to maintain close proximity to you especially as your fire started to intensify, but we had to wait till each of you was ready."

Selah witnessed the glow on Tony's skin, like a warm rippling wildfire. She closed her eyes trying to shake the vision away, but it remained. "Daniel had the abilities of swiftness, stealth, and speaking God's truth and divine messages, though these abilities will now be passed on to someone else."

Selah's heart ached, a feeling of numbness covered her mind. Daniel couldn't really be gone. She sniffled and turned her attention back to Michael.

"Jaidyn, your abilities are focused on the healing arts. You can heal to the point of resurrecting life but only when allowed by God; you can calm the spirit of any living thing, and see true emotions clearly."

Selah looked at her best friend, concentrating on the arm nearest to her, the air fluttering around her, and Jaidyn's arm began to radiate a calming bluish-purple hue with a soft iridescence. Her glow was the most serene.

"Could she bring Daniel back?" Selah blurted.

"Unfortunately, if she tried now, what would come back would not be Daniel's pure soul."

Selah's hope sank like a stone.

"Finally." Michael caught the grief in Selah's eyes. "Selah, your abilities to analyze, strategically solve problems, and sense when something is wrong gives you a great upper hand when fighting for your friends and family."

"None of that helped me tonight," Selah interrupted. "I had no idea Daniel would be shot. Shouldn't I have sensed that?"

Michael's shoulders slumped. "Your abilities need to be focused and strengthened. You are working against forces that are dark, clouding objectivity at times. It is not your fault Selah. We should have known, since each one of you is connected to one of us. Our connection since the day we blessed you with God's purpose and brought your souls to your parents. We were here to guard and protect you, to bless your lives, and equip you for the darkness to come. I failed twice now, but you, you did not."

●   CHAPTER 25   ●

MICHAEL

"What are we then, some kind of superheroes?" Tony quipped.

Their mortal minds would have a hard time processing all this, but Michael pressed on. "No, not exactly superheroes, but, yes, you have supernatural abilities most human beings do not have. It may take some time for you to understand and see the spiritual realm, but when you do it will help accept why you have been anointed as chosen vessels of God. You are here, at this date and time to save your city."

"And what exactly are we saving Gailton from?" Tony asked. Michael watched him shift his weight, likely steeling himself for the answer. He uncrossed his arms from his chest.

"Sure, there is some crazy stuff happening around here, but can't the police take care of it?"

Michael smiled. "The police cannot see what is happening behind the scenes; if they could, they would be terrified. Only you, the Chosen, us..." He gestured, including all the Archangels. "...and the other Angels in this jurisdiction are equipped to defeat the enemies that remain unseen from the human eye. Like that man, Baleel that shot Daniel tonight. He was an incubus and has now been sent back to hell dreaming about his next meal. He may have looked human, but he was a greater demon. He walks the Earth encouraging violence and hate."

Selah and Jaidyn hung their heads, defeated, but not Tony. Michael recalled the night Uriel went to rescue Tony from the accident that took his parents. Tony was a child when it happened. He had told the cops someone had stopped their car. He described the demon, Abaddon to a *T*—Abaddon, the King of the Army of Locust, the Destroyer and Lucifer's right-hand man. The police later told Tony that the man was a drunk and that he had been driving recklessly, trying to explain that that was what stopped the car. Michael sensed that Tony still had his suspicions. Michael, though, was still uncertain why Abaddon was sent to kill Tony and his parents, a job that seemed a little lowly for his talents.

"We are in charge of keeping Lucifer and his followers in check. They have parameters. They are fully aware of how far they can go, though they continue to tiptoe around the boundaries that have been set. You," he addressed the Chosen, "have all been under God's protection along with all those who have accepted His help. Unfortunately, this doesn't keep evil from running rampant. It isn't foolproof, but, even with death as a possible outcome, it means Heaven for those who choose. I am sorry it didn't protect your father, Selah, or your parents, Tony. Lucifer and his followers are intent to kill, steal and destroy everything in which God loves. God doles out justice accordingly, and though He is slow to anger, He will not be tested. So, when these sycophants meander where they shouldn't God's wrath and justice is swift, that I can assure you. You have seen Lucifer face-to-face, and tonight is no exception to the other evils you will later witness."

"We have seen the Devil face-to-face?" Selah scoffed.

"Yes, in his club, AfterBurn," Michael assured, but before Michael could continue Tony interrupted.

"I have watched as friend after friend became addicted to drugs coming out of that club. You're telling us this place is the hideout for the Devil himself? I know Marcus and Judas have played their part in all of this, too. What about them? Are they part of this evil you're talking about? Because Sean is in the middle of this mess now and is one of the main reasons I took this bartending job, not knowing I was working for the Devil."

Selah gave him a sincere smile.

Michael answered, "Yes, we know Luc Vega as Lucifer." Each of the Chosen gawked at him as he continued. "Marcus and Judas are known by different names and faces." He looked at Uriel, who nodded at Michael to continue. This was going to sound absurd to them. "We know them as Beelzebub and Asmodeus. Beelzebub was the second seraphim to fall from Heaven with Lucifer, Asmodeus is also a former seraphim. Uriel once worked closely with both of them. That is the only way we knew who we were dealing with when we first heard about them. I warn you though, Marcus, or Beelzebub, is cruel and cunning—he is greed incarnate. Judas, or Asmodeus, is the wanton one. He plays on the lustful desires of man."

Selah stood. Jaidyn's shock kept her plastered to the couch. Tony continued to shake his head.

Selah retorted, "How the hell is this even possible? Isn't Lucifer supposed to be in charge of Hell or something? What would he want with our little town?"

"He wants you," Michael said pointedly. "To destroy all of you. He has been prowling from town to town throughout the millennia, influencing and encouraging all kinds of debauchery. Before, he walked only in his spiritual form—him and his associates. It was twenty years ago when we found out he was planning on taking on a disguise, a human form. He finally accomplished it two years afterward; though we are still unsure of exactly how he did it. As soon as Heaven got word of what was happening, God created each of you, then dispatched us here to train you. Together we could protect your town, your people and destroy Lucifer's fleshly form.

It would have been no issue for me to send him back where he came from if he were still prowling around in his spiritual form, however, now that he wears flesh only mortals can destroy his human form, and then we angels will dispatch his spirit."

"But you guys wear human forms now, can't you do it?" Jaidyn addressed Michael.

"While we wear human forms, we are still only spiritual beings. Our forms are more a play on light and shadow, like a glamour. You are of human blood, with the anointing of the Most High; only you can defeat him in his flesh." Michael wished he could spare them this burden, but the crossroad lay before them. Would they take up the cause or run in fear?

"I, for one am ready to do something," Jaidyn declared up from the couch. "I am tired of seeing people I love hurt by this man. Daniel is gone, and we will never get him back. We can't lose Sean too. What do we need to do?"

Her bravery shone brightly, but Michael knew this next stage was not going to be easy for them.

"You will need to train with us. You will have to come here every day after school and before your work hours. We will teach you all you need to know.

It won't be easy. We will have to stretch you in ways you can't imagine. Though when you are done, you will be able to not only spot evil in the spiritual realm but defeat it."

Raphael added with her calming presence, reassuring their hearts. "This will be overwhelming, but together we can see amazing things come out of this." She looked at Jaidyn and then Selah. "You will get Sean back."

Selah looked at Jaidyn, at her sullen expression. Daniel was gone, but the resolve on her face determined they would not lose her brother. Tony looked far more eager than all of them. The Chosen said together, "When do we start?"

That question was the easiest to answer. Michael looked at each of them with pride; their strength of character made him clearly understand why God had chosen them. "Tomorrow afternoon."

● CHAPTER 26 ●

SELAH

One minute you think you know your life's story and the next you are wondering if maybe you've lost your mind altogether.

Selah had questioned her version of reality after the Angels revealed the truth to them. Two weeks had passed since then; they had been practicing every day and night, and she was finally beginning to feel stronger, maybe even strong enough to take on a man like Luc Vega. Knowing he wasn't a man at all, but Lucifer himself, steeled her determination to continue to train with every spare hour she had.

Selah watched Jaidyn take another swing at Raphael, the trails of lightning-quick movements were still something to get used to. It was as if knowing the truth of who they were had unleashed something in each of them.

Tony, who was always strong no doubt, could now crush bones with his grip and took great care to harness the holy fire he had been gifted with. She questioned why she never recognized Tony's gift before. Jaidyn's was believable—she was always trying to help someone who was hurting—but now that she thought of it, she had never seen Tony around fire.

Selah was stronger and faster also. She could see an opponent's purpose, their strategy, before they even made a move, instinctively knowing how to counterattack whatever was about to come her way. So far, she had been undefeated by her friends, though she knew that would not matter when it came to their supernatural foes.

Tony and Uriel were battling it out on the mat, using all the mixed martial arts they had trained with, including some Krav Maga defensive tactics. Tony's prior strength gave him a lethal edge; with the intense training, he now had the strength and power to strike a man dead.

Daniel's absence was a constant reminder that they weren't facing humans, but demons, pushing them all to learn these deadly arts more quickly. Maybe it was fear, maybe determination, or possibly both that made Tony and Selah train at night even after their shifts at work. Their movements were becoming so precise and quick Selah wondered if their opponents would even see them coming. Even with her ability to see Tony's strategy, it was hard to determine where a blow was going to land. She grinned to herself as she watched Jaidyn and Tony and carried on punching and kicking the dummy in front of her.

She stopped to wipe sweat from her brow when she spotted Tony and Uriel taking a break too. Seemed like every free moment she had in Tony's presence her eyes would fall on him. She tried not to stare too much, but when he began to wipe the sweat from his face and arms she noticed the tension in his muscles—muscles that were now far more defined. She averted her eyes back to her dummy and blushed at her thoughts. They had not talked much since she kissed him at the club. She wasn't sure if it was guilt with Daniel being gone, even though she had enjoyed the kiss. Knowing her ex-boyfriend and longtime friend was never coming back put a damper on the joy she wanted desperately to feel; it could have been the new knowledge of their purpose, or perhaps with all the confusion it was easier to avoid it altogether. She played with the idea of asking Tony about what happened, but every time she was about to, she froze. What happened to the confidence that night?

Jaidyn was over at one of the smaller mats working on healing. Raphael had brought in a dog that had been scheduled that day to be euthanized. The sable German Shepherd looked like she was already on her way out. Jaidyn stroked the beautiful dog's head, being as gentle as she could, then bent over to whisper something in her ear. Even with how far away Selah was standing she could see the life come back into the dog's eyes. Jaidyn moved her hands to the dogs engorged belly and whispered a prayer.

A gentle glow of pure golden light began shimmering and sparkling, but a mist of pure black, something dark and sinister poured out of the dog, fighting against the light. Jaidyn twisted her hands around the darkness, seizing it, then eradicated the darkness with showers of golden light exploding away from her hand. The dog's tail began to wag, then she stood up, looking younger and more filled with life. A dog with a second chance.

Selah and Tony both walked toward them at the same time.

"Wow, that was incredible Jay!" Selah affirmed as she got down to the dog's level and scratched her behind both fuzzy ears. The dog was definitely smiling.

Tony got down next to Selah and looked at her while he rubbed the dog's back.

"What are we gonna name her?" he questioned.

"We can't keep her; she probably has owners," Jaidyn said, looking to Raphael with a questioning glance.

"Actually, this little lady was brought to us as a stray. Someone had left the poor girl to die."

Selah and Jaidyn both gasped, sadly shocked.

Tony hooked his arm around the dog's neck and hugged her.

"I will take her. If that is okay, of course. My grandma needs a dog when I am not there, especially with Grandpa being sick. Would that be okay?"

Who could say no to that?

"That's fine with me. What do you think girls?"

Selah and Jaidyn smiled and nodded.

"Yeah, sounds good. What are you going to name her though?" Jaidyn asked.

"I was thinking Jael, after the woman in the Bible who took down a whole army by killing one man." With his smile of pride, how could they object? "We can call her Elle for short, so we don't confuse her with Jay." He winked at Jaidyn.

"Well, that settles it then, welcome to the family Elle," Selah said as she scratched behind Elle's left ear. She looked up at Selah with those sweet brown puppy dog eyes. "She is going to melt your grandma's heart. Be careful."

They all laughed.

They went on to finish their training while Raph took Elle for a walk. Selah's heart felt lighter since watching Jaidyn bring life back to Elle. Her hope grew. Maybe, just maybe, with all this training they could actually help bring more life to this town and destroy the darkness, just like Jaidyn just did. She understood it would not be nearly as easy.

In mid-thought Tony caught her eye. He was across the room doing pull-ups. She smiled innocently as he dismounted and began walking her way.

When he reached her, he opened his mouth then shut it, sighed, then started again. "Selah, I think maybe tomorrow we should meet up. I have wanted to talk to ya since AfterBurn, to be honest, I just didn't know what to say." He looked uneasy. "You think we could go for a ride or something?" His deep, sincere gaze eased her confused mind. She knew she couldn't put this off any longer.

"Yeah." She looked down at her feet. "That would be great. Tomorrow around 5:00 p.m.?"

"I have work tomorrow night at the club but not till 8:00 p.m. so that'll be perfect. See you then? I'll pick you up at your house." He began walking backward, heading back to the pull-up bars.

"Okay, see you then," Selah confirmed with a chuckle.

They had fifteen more minutes of intense training till they could leave. Jaidyn and Selah luckily had another Friday night off together, they planned to go to Selah's house where Elizabeth was desperately waiting for "girl time." Tony headed out for another Friday night shift at AfterBurn.

Selah wondered how hard it must be to go back to the place where your friend had been shot, remain "undercover" and still do your job. Tony's strength wasn't only physical. His heart was full of courage too.

CHAPTER 27

TONY

After packing himself up from training and grabbing Elle's leash, Tony waved a goodbye to everyone. Elle strutted with pride now that she was healed. Jaidyn's abilities were incredible, the power to heal and give new life. In comparison, Tony felt completely inept. His fire abilities conveyed destruction, a power meant to destroy, or at most, provide heat. He kind of envied Jaidyn. Understanding each of them had been given different gifts for different reasons didn't help Tony feel any less inadequate.

Tonight, Gabriel followed him home since Tony's motorcycle was not equipped to hold a dog. Once he thanked Gabriel for bringing her, he headed toward the front door. His grandma bought this updated mobile home right after his parents had passed away; they needed the extra room so they could keep Tony with them. No matter how small it seemed, this house felt like home. He appreciated that his grandparents bought it just to provide for him. With all they had done over these many years, Tony hoped to one day have the means to pay them back for their love and kindness.

His grandma, May, was sitting where she always did, in her soft purple microfiber recliner. She was knitting away at some crocheting project. She peered over her gold rimmed bifocals at him. "Hey hun, whatcha got there?" Her gaze fell on Elle. "That is one beautiful dog."

"Well, Gram I brought her here for you and Grandpa, so you have company while I am working late at night. I promise to take care of her, so there is no need for you to do anything but take care of Grandpa. I will pick up a crate for her before work for her to sleep in tonight. Can she stay?"

He encouragingly walked Elle over to his Grandma. She set her sweet head on his grandmother's lap, and when Elle twitched her eyebrow and gave a sweet sigh, Gram was won over.

"Oh, what a precious girl." She stroked her soft coat with a grin. "My boy, you didn't have to buy her for us. We will be fine. Would hate to have you spend your hard-earned money. Though she is a darling." Gram rubbed around her ears just like Selah had.

Tony smiled.

"Oh no Gram, she was a stray. Can you believe, someone had abandoned her and left her to die? Jaidyn, Selah's best friend, you know, the redhead, she was able to help her and I asked if we could keep her. I know how you feel about abandoned animals." It was true, none of the cats in the neighborhood lived in their house, but Grandma was always nursing stray cats or feeding abandoned kittens. It kinda explained why Tony was there too, a lost kid, in need of care.

Gram's smile grew. She got up, took the leash from Tony and unlatched it. Elle was so calm, though her tail wagged with excitement.

"She must come meet Gramps."

Tony watched as Elle walked with his grandma down the hall and turned into Grandpa's room. Tony followed. Elle went up on her hind legs, nudging

Gramps, who lay there motionless, introducing herself. Tony watched as the same light Jaidyn had used to heal Elle began swirling around his grandpa. A smile grew on his grandpa's face, for the first time in months.

Well look at that!

"She has to stay now. Grandpa made a new friend." Gram had turned to Tony, tears of joy welling in her eyes. "I haven't seen him light up like that since you guys fixed that last cycle together, right before his stroke. She will do just fine here hun, just fine." She quickly turned back toward Gramps as he suddenly tried to sit up in bed.

"My sweet angel here does she have a name?" Gramps sputtered. Grandma grabbed at her chest.

Tony came farther into the room. "Her name is Jael, Gramps, or we can call her Elle for short." Grandpa began to pet her, and more of that life energy hummed around her and Gramps. *How is this possible?* Tony looked up toward the ceiling, knowing only God could do such a thing. Tears fell silently down Tony's face.

Gram was overtaken in a full joyous cry.

This was a miracle of epic proportions. Since his grandfather had a stroke three years ago, the same year Selah lost her dad, Gramps had not moved or talked since.

Gram tentatively moved in closer to Gramps. Slowly, his hand shaking, he reached up and touched Gram's face. "I have missed you, my girl."

Tony quietly backed out of the room to give them privacy. He was shaken but in a good way. Elle's healing influence had thoroughly impacted his whole family. He was absolutely convinced she belonged nowhere else. Tony thanked God above as he tried to ground himself from such an emotional high.

He managed to get himself dressed for work. He headed out early to get the crate for Elle, being sure to take Gram's little SUV.

When he made it back, he walked in to find Grandpa sitting in his recliner. Tony dropped the crate and almost crushed his toes. *Holy God above!* Tony shook his head in disbelief and walked quickly over to Gramps, wrapping him up in a bear hug. "Oh man, I have missed you Gramps."

Tony willed himself not to cry. The huge smile, however, he could not contain. He heard his grandma frantically cooking in the kitchen. She hadn't made Grandpa a real meal in a long time. Ensure drinks and soft foods had been his diet for so long.

"Oh, my boy," Gramps said. "It is good to be back to myself. I don't know how it happened, but I know this girl has something to do with it." Gramps looked down at Elle, who was resting her head on his armrest as he stroked her head. "I will never forget this. God only knows how much I have wanted to come back to you and Gram." Tears pooled in his worn eyes.

Tony's chest tightened with overwhelming gladness. This was not how he expected tonight to go, though it was at the top of the list as one of the best nights of his life. There was nothing quite as miraculous as having someone you thought was gone breathe with new life.

"Gramps, I hate to leave, but I have to go into work tonight. Promise you'll go easy on Gram, she may have a heart attack from sheer happiness if you're not careful." He winked at his grandpa who gave a hearty laughed.

"Glad you haven't changed one bit my boy." He smiled warmly at Tony. "Elle and I will take care of her, don't you worry."

Tony made sure to put the crate together before he left. On his way out the door, he looked back one more time on a scene he never thought he would see again, grateful.

CHAPTER 28

SELAH

Selah and Jaidyn arrived at her house and walked in to her mom waiting on the couch.

When Elizabeth saw Selah and Jaidyn, all sweaty and in their workout gear, she asked, "What have you girls been up to?"

Selah remembered she had lied to her mom about their new routine. She wasn't sure if she was going to ever be able to tell her mom the real truth, and it felt like every time she turned around she was making up some story to cover strange truths that were beyond human logic, even her mom's.

"Seems like every time I see you girls now, you both look so grown up. Today you girls are glowing.

It makes me jealous of your youth." She laughed it off.

"We just started a new workout routine a couple weeks ago. We have been going after school, usually before work or when I am having a hard time sleeping." Selah answered.

"Oh, that's great. Where are you working out?"

A seemingly innocent question.

Selah thought carefully. If she told her mom they were going to the local gym, only to have Mom try to get a membership, she would quickly discover that they had never been going there, and Selah would be in deep trouble.

"Oh...um, well, Tony lets us use his grandparents' little shed. He turned it into a gym not too long ago." Selah surprised herself. She pleaded with God above to forgive her for deceiving her mom. She honestly didn't know what else to do.

"I have always liked Tony," Elizabeth stated. "How are his grandma and grandpa doing?"

Phew! Selah was grateful for the change of subject.

"Same as always. We don't see his grandma much except to say a quick hi, but she seems okay." Selah's guilt felt like a leaded blanket. She needed to go see Tony's grandma not just because she didn't need another lie stacked up on the pile she had already accumulated, but because she really did like Tony's gram.

"Good, his grandma is a sweet lady." Elizabeth moved her legs on the couch, to make room for them. "Are you girls still up for a movie night?"

Selah desperately desired to go to bed; she was exhausted. Jaidyn looked beat too, but they weren't backing out on Mom not after all the lying.

"Yeah, Mom, just give us a minute to get changed. Will you make the popcorn?"

She headed to her room while keeping eye contact with her mom. Elizabeth smiled at her.

"Sure kiddo. You girls can pick the movie tonight too."

Selah couldn't even think right now; her mind was so numbingly exhausted from all the work she had been doing this week. She hurt in places she didn't even know you could hurt, and by the groans Jaidyn let out as she sat on the bed, she got the impression she felt the same.

Selah never imagined she would one day have muscles, at least not ones you could actually see. She stared at herself for a second as she undressed. Her body had changed so much since they'd started training, like she had been weight training for years, when it had only been a couple weeks.

Selah caught a glimpse of Jaidyn. They were beginning to look like toned professional athletes, the one's she had once been so jealous of on TV during the summer Olympics. Selah felt great, but it seemed so surreal. Even her glow had started to even out to a soft, low, white glow that surrounded all her skin. She looked like she had recently had a deep detoxifying spa day rather than the light show her glow would do before, flickering off and on all the time. Jaidyn still had the subtle blueish-purple sparkle of a glow. One of the major parts of their training was learning to control their light, especially when their emotions intensified. For Selah, it was much needed with how often her glow had unwillingly flared before.

"Jaidyn, I meant to tell you in the car, but I am just so tired I forgot." They had ridden together all day today, to school, training, and back to Selah's, but she never got to tell her. "Tony is coming tomorrow night. He wants to talk about our night at AfterBurn."

Jaidyn looked sincerely at her. "Are you nervous?" She smiled as she slipped on her fuzzy fleece socks to match the pajamas she'd brought for tonight's sleepover.

"Yeah, I mean, it was a crazy night. I am still trying to grasp that Daniel isn't coming back from this. That he is actually really gone. When I walk on campus I keep expecting to see him." Her voice hitched. "Yet, the kiss with Tony felt amazing. I feel so guilty even thinking about it. And honestly, I just don't know what to say."

Selah fumbled with her pajama top while trying to continue. "I shocked myself that night when I kissed him. One second he was complimenting my glow and the next I am kissing him, then the screams, and Daniel dead, then to find out we are some strange version of superheroes." She took a deep breath. "How do I tell Tony that I like him, that I would love to date him when we have all this going on? The pressure to defeat evil—Lucifer of all evils! It still sounds so absurd. When I really think about it, I wonder if it is smart to tell Tony how I feel. We have everything else we should be focused on." Selah, deflated, flopped down on her bed, face to the mattress.

Was she being selfish wanting to be with Tony while all of this was going on? Would they really even be able to have a relationship with all the training, both of their jobs, and Selah still juggling school? Where would they even find the time? She was still spinning wheels in her own mind when Jaidyn began talking.

"Don't you think it would make things more awkward if you don't tell him how you feel and still have to train together every day? You know, God has grace for all of humanity, that includes both of you. I don't think He would be upset by you telling Tony how you feel and dating him even with all this outside stuff going on. Who knows, it could make you both work harder, being together and fighting the same evil. I have seen enough prime time TV to tell you it can work." She smiled encouragingly at Selah. "Besides, Say, I know Tony is head over heels for you. It would probably be way more hurtful pretending your feelings aren't there."

Selah glared at her wise friend, hating that she was right. "You know when you're right, you're right." She laughed, grabbed her blanket off her bed as she got up, and both of them went to the living room.

"Also," Jaidyn whispered to her in the hall, "your mom likes him so that's a plus." She rose both her eyebrows suggestively. Selah rolled her eyes at her crazy friend.

"You're incorrigible!" She bumped her hip against Jaidyn's as she walked over to the kitchen to get some sodas. Jaidyn grabbed her seat on one side of the couch. Elizabeth had just finished making the popcorn, spraying on some olive oil and covering it with a few shakes of garlic salt.

Selah plopped down next to Jaidyn in the middle and Mom shook up the big bowl of popcorn, then sat next to Selah.

"What do you want to watch?" Selah asked Jaidyn, hoping secretly she would pick something that wasn't a love story. She had her own romantic drama playing in her head right now.

"*Pride and Prejudice and Zombies.*" Leave it to Jaidyn; she did not disappoint. Selah scrolled through

Netflix on their SmartTV and found what she was looking for.

"It's not super scary, right?" Elizabeth asked.

Mom was a chicken when it came to scary movies, though so were Selah and Jaidyn. Jaidyn laughed, then answered. "No, it is a little suspenseful but not that bad. If you get too scared you can dump the popcorn on Say."

Selah rolled her eyes at Jaidyn as her mom and Jaidyn chuckled together, then mouthed, "Traitor."

Jaidyn stuffed her mouth full of popcorn as the movie began to play.

●   CHAPTER 29   ●

TONY

Tony pulled into the AfterBurn parking lot on his Harley. He parked his baby in the back near the dumpster; from this spot he could check on it periodically from the open back door of the club.

Uriel gave him an acknowledging nod as he walked through the front doors. They had done well keeping their relationship from the knowing eyes of Luc Vega. Tony had mastered the ability to completely shut down the glowing fire in his veins. Luckily, for him it was never a problem for him like it had been for Selah. But he kept his ability to alight objects under lock and key while he worked at the club. He did like having fun with it outside the club, like when he would light the gas stove for Grams without her knowledge.

Uriel's eyes followed him as he walked by. Tony had just started becoming comfortable with eyes on him. It was far more comforting knowing it was Uriel. While Uriel was keeping a watchful eye on him, Tony kept a watchful eye on Sean. Since the day he started at AfterBurn he had tried to keep a tight watch on Sean, though he was beginning to see things he knew he would have to tell Selah about.

Sean was working tonight till midnight on Uriel's bouncer crew. Which meant Uriel would keep him out of trouble for a bit. Earlier this week, during AfterBurn's "Thirties and Up" night, Sean somehow squeaked his way in alongside Judas, who just happened to be working that night in the back office, doing God only knows what.

In the couple weeks since Tony had come to work at the club, he still had not figured out what the heck that guy did for Luc. He knew Marcus was Luc's top Doxy dealer, but Judas wasn't showing off his talents for the whole world to see.

That same night, Sean had gone in the back with Judas. He came out with a black trash bag filled with what looked to be blocks. Sean left the club with the bag and returned empty handed.

Tony hoped that Sean was unknowingly helping Judas launder whatever money they got from this venue and Luc's other ventures. Otherwise, if he knew what he was doing, he didn't understand the severity of what would happen if he got caught. Over these past couple weeks, Tony had a sickening feeling that some of Luc's other interests included illegal weapons, smuggling and sales. While Tony had not seen a transaction take place in the wild flashing lights of the club, he often witnessed Judas and a few of the uglier bouncers bring in suitcases, taking them directly to the back office, only for those same suitcases to leave with low-level crime lords. Tony knew a few of them by face, their territories on the other side of Gailton. It just proved there were a lot of sinister works going on in this club.

Sean was currently lounging in the VIP booth with Judas, Marcus, Quinn, and Anne-Marie. He took another line of Doxy and looked rather content. Quinn was rubbing his back and laughing at something one of the other girls sitting near them had said.

Tony rolled his eyes, shocked and disgusted at seeing just how much Sean had fallen into his addiction. It seemed so unnatural that Sean showed absolutely no signs of anything being wrong; the only outward sign something was going on was his growing muscles, as if he were taking steroids instead of Doxy. He wasn't bulky by any means, but they had grown enough to be disturbing. Sean was beginning to look like a prizefighter.

Despite the back-office shenanigans of the weeks and nights prior, tonight was business as usual: bodies swayed on the dance floor, music played so loudly you couldn't hear the person next to you, with the artificial fog and lights flashing. The bar was busy as usual, all nameless faces. Tony only had to fill drinks for the VIP section twice. The night was coming to an end but all Tony kept thinking about was the night of Daniel's death. There wasn't even an indication that anything violent had happened here. The altercation had only been three feet from where Tony stood, and the exact spot where Daniel had taken a bullet to the chest, then dropped dead. There was no evidence to prove Daniel had ever been there. No bloodstains, no bullet fragments. Nothing.

Tony overheard one of the other bartenders hushed a whisper to a customer that, Luc apparently "disposed of" the guy who shot the kid. The memories and frustrations of that night haunted him even if there were no physical reminders. However, his pain wasn't about to keep him from bartending in this crazy club, because he'd made a vow to help destroy Luc Vega.

Luc rarely made an appearance outside of the back office. As soon as the club lights came on, Luc hid and would not be seen till the club closed.

As Tony scrubbed down the bar one last time and tucked the rag into his back pocket, he spotted Luc watching the whole room from the open doorway of his office. The office lights were out, but Tony could faintly make out the outline of his statuesque form. Luc watched the crowd like a lion stalking his next meal: still, silent, and hidden. Tony moved to help a customer, trying to remember to hold tight on his glow. He could feel Luc's dark stare boring into him. He didn't let it deter him from doing his work. While Tony may know the truth of his evil incarnate status, it only made Tony more determined to be strong in his presence.

Tony continued to mix drinks he would never drink, laugh and chat with clubgoers, putting on his best customer service smile. He kept up this pace easily until his shift was over. He watched the crowd dwindle and trickle out the club's front doors. He finished up by washing a few remaining glasses, then drying them.

Uriel came up to the bar. "Hey, kid, good job tonight. I know this isn't as easy for you as you make it seem." He cocked a half smile, then slipped into a serious gaze. "Luc was watching tonight. Not sure if he was watching the floor or the workers, but he is no fool. Be extra cautious."

"Will do." He grinned at Uriel. "Thanks."

"No problem. See ya later, kid." The next moment Uriel was already out the front door, though it didn't take Tony long to follow. Then he heard his name.

"Hey Tone!" Sean called from the VIP section he had gone back to occupying once his shift was over.

"Hey, what's up?"

"Nothing, just saying hi. Tell my sister I say hi too." He laughed, glancing at Quinn, who grabbed his hand and laughed. "She's a prude you know."

Tony pursed his lips and shook his head. He had never heard Sean talk about his sister in such a cruel way. He would never be so cutting.

"Sean, stop before you say something you'll regret." Tony turned on his heel and walked away disgusted and disappointed. He obviously needed to help Sean before he ruined his relationship with his own family.

"I don't know what you see in her, Tone. She makes white bread seem interesting. She is so predictable and you won't get anywhere with her, man," he yelled with a chuckle.

Tony turned, glaring at him over his shoulder. Only three more steps and he would be out the door.

"Why even bother if you can't get what you want out of it." Sean looked at Quinn with greedy desire. It was definitely not love Tony saw in his eyes.

Tony fully faced Sean from across the room. "Well, I don't need what you do, Sean, to be happy. Maybe rethink your life a bit, brother, before it's too late." Before the situation could escalate or go to blows, Tony turned, walking right out the door. He didn't care to hear anything else that might come from Sean's foolish drug-induced brain.

Tony could feel someone else's eyes on him again. He scanned the area when he got onto his motorcycle and saw nothing. He put on his helmet and brought the engine to life. He needed a ride through the back roads of Gailton in the cool wind of the night. Hopefully, the peace and tranquility of the quiet streets would clear the anger that was rising in his chest. He took off from AfterBurn's parking lot like a bat out of hell.

CHAPTER 30

LUCIFER

Luc had always felt trapped in the confines of Earth, to rule from the underbelly of this "Eden". Humanity had no idea what they had missed out on. Lucifer often relished in the emotions Adam and Eve felt the moment they realized their loss. He would go back and play it over in his mind, enjoying it like a fine wine; their misery, shame, and guilt. They had never seen his treachery coming. The fools!

Ever since the Fall of Man, humans were oblivious to the ways in which he used them. They would never know how much fun it was for him to play with their fragile souls. He was a connoisseur of those who wanted power and prestige; He often would possess kings, and rulers of the realm like

Tyre, Herod, and Hitler. There were only a few humans who held such destruction in their hearts and an unquenchable thirst for power. It was almost too easy to slip into such mortals and take on their lives, because their sin was so close to his own, pride.

Lucifer smiled remembering.

This new body, however, had no master. The soul had been long gone when the necromancer awakened Lucifer into this new form. It wasn't a bad fit. Sure, the body was a little older than he had desired but still highly useful. The chiseled features were pleasing to the female eye, yet intimidating to other males. His salt-and-pepper hair and finely trimmed beard portrayed a look of power. The body was fit like a Roman soldier from the time of Caesar.

He hid in the doorway of his darkened office, his eyes following the writhing bodies of young women bent on lust and debauchery, and observed the demons ready to have their way with them. He caught Sean Moore, who was sitting with Marcus and Judas. Those two peons where lucky they still lived most days. When Judas asked about Sean working at the club, he was all too glad to jump at the chance at keeping one of the Chosen's loved ones so close.

Since the day Selah was born, Luc knew of her existence. It just so happened she was born on the day he entered this new body. Luc's countdown clock started the minute she took her first breath. It ticked away the time he had left to acquire new territory. Constantly, it ticked at the back of his mind.

Selah wouldn't make a move against him, not with her brother so close to his lackey demons. Luc smiled as he watched Quinn with Sean. He was rather proud of her. She was a power-hungry succubus and made herself available to take on the task of entertaining the young man. Marcus was quick-witted enough to get Sean hooked on the Doxy as well.

It surprised Luc that Sean had survived the constant dosing. Although, it bothered Luc that there was something about Sean that changed the dark forces in his club, like a ripple in water. It was if Angelic forces were in his midst. Luc's biggest fear was stolen time. He needed this plan of his to work, but with every new recruit's death, his plan fell through. Sean was his only promising candidate. If he could keep the Angels from interfering, he might be able to pull it off.

His eyes caught on Tony. Luc thought back to the night Abaddon was sent to kill the Chosen and their parents. He was supposed to find out their identities and report back to Luc. Prior to leaving that night to find the Chosen, Abaddon told Luc some of his suspicions. Together they had concocted a plan to destroy each of them before they could become a threat. Unfortunately, Luc had never heard from Abaddon after that night. If that lowlife was back in Hell Luc wouldn't hear the truth from him until he went back to Hell himself, and he didn't plan on doing that anytime soon.

Luc had heard that Tony's parents were killed in a drunk driving accident. If Tony had been one of the Chosen, he couldn't have planned that any better himself, except that Tony would have been killed too.

Every time Luc got closer to finding out who the other Chosen were or how many of them there could possibly be, the information disappeared or was snatched away. Clenching his jaw, he ground his teeth. Luc knew full well that it was his Father. That it was God and his miserable army of Angels that were continually making him into a fool.

He arched a brow while watching Tony. If this young man was anything close to a Chosen vessel, Luc was sure he would have sensed something by now. Granted, there was something about that kid. Luc could taste the grief and loss rising from his spirit, but that was common with the amount of loss he must have experienced.

Tony continued to take drink orders, wiping down the counter in between and flashing his generous smile to the customers. Luc was determined to find out if there was any substance to this kid other than being an unlucky bastard.

Luc's gaze swept over the rest of the club. Uriel was as stoic as he always was. Luc found Uriel's name to be comical. It was the name of one of his brothers, although his brother was far more beautiful, and full of glorious burning light. Luc tried to imagine if his brother was ever human and what form he would likely take. Most likely bright, lean, and lethal, not some stocky guy wrapped in dark tattoos, over-muscled with an ugly scar to boot.

Uriel was one of Luc's most efficient workers, although he didn't catch Baleel, whom Luc had sent to shoot Daniel. Daniel had been easy to spot as a Chosen One, and when Daniel acted like he had no idea what Baleel was referring to Baleel shot him anyway. Luc wondered if maybe having demons at the front door would keep out the riffraff. Lucifer chuckled darkly to himself; demons were the riffraff.

Baleel and his antics were easy enough to erase anyway. The night of the shooting, the Angel powers Luc sensed at times were far more potent among the crowd. He had watched Selah that night, believing the Angels were most likely with her. When the shot rang out, he had to direct all attention to the horde of terrified humans intermingled with demons and keep them from destroying each other, and the cops from shutting him down for good.

So many questions remained unanswered. Who were the Angels? And how long did he have before they foiled his current plans. Could Sean be one of the Chosen? He was, after all, a sibling of a Chosen One. Did he have the same abilities as his sister, and was he just as clueless as she was about those abilities? Or was it Tony, the kid bartender with the bad luck? Luc retreated back to his office, shutting the door, then turning on the lights. This was not going to be solved tonight. He needed to get back to work on the latest shipment of his demon swords and weapons.

Months ago, he'd begun preparing the Fallen to fight these blessed unnamed mortals. The Fallen had at one time been Angels with him in Heaven. They had chosen to follow him. While he could hate the lot of them because they were all imbeciles, they were at least loyal. They needed no preparations as far as fighting skills but they did need weapons that could severely wound an Angel of Heaven and kill any of the Chosen they came in contact with.

Lucifer's blood, part Angelic and partly filled with his iniquity, became the lethal ingredient used to make such weapons. He commissioned the generals of Hell to design and forge them. Now, he needed to figure out how to bring them into the realm of the living. In Hell, Luc's generals were currently the Keepers of the Dead; they helped keep Hell's chaos minimal while Lucifer explored his new form and tried to conquer new territory here on Earth. The generals themselves couldn't cross over, nor could Luc unless he wanted to stay in Hell. It would take a mortal tainted by Hell to crossover and come back.

Getting a mortal to walk into Hell was not an easy task.

Sean! If he could live through the varying doses of Doxy, the demon blood in Doxy surely made him tainted, and likely strong enough to do the task. This could work. He sat back with a wicked smirk.

Now, how do I convince Sean to walk into the pits of Hell?

CHAPTER 31

SELAH

Selah stared into the full-length mirror, convincing her courage not to give out on her tonight. She was trying hard not to overthink, but that task seemed impossible. Every distraction she tried earlier in the day—cleaning, drawing, reading, homework—nothing seemed to keep her from worrying over what would be said between her and Tony this evening.

She knew Tony was on his way, and her anxiety heightened at every passing minute.

His Harley was hard to miss as it rumbled down her street and pulled up to the house. Quickly, she grabbed her leather moto jacket. When Tony suggested a ride together, she couldn't refuse. Tonight's weather was perfect for it. She loved riding on motorcycles. Maybe one day she would learn to drive one herself. Before she could make it out the door, Elizabeth spoke from the hallway as she made her way to the kitchen. "Tell Tony I said hello!" Then she winked at Selah. *Did she just wink?*

"Okay, Mom!" Selah let out an exasperated sigh and flew out the door. She made it to the end of the driveway when Tony turned off his motorcycle.

"Aren't we going for a ride?" She could hear the disappointment in her own voice.

"Yeah, but when I thought more about it, motorcycle rides aren't great for conversations. Instead, I thought maybe we could ride in your car."

She looked at her big white beast of a car and signaled for Tony to wait a second as she ran back in to grab her keys. Riding in her car was not nearly as fun as a motorcycle ride, but it was still fun to cruise in. She was able to grab her keys and head back out the door before her mom could hear her. Selah was glad to avoid more innuendos from her.

"Okay, let's go." She walked to the driver side. Tony's eyes sparked as he smiled at her over the top of her car, setting her nerves ablaze, running a satisfying shock all down her spine. She got behind the steering wheel and started the car, trying to avoid glancing at him. She could feel the heat from her chest to her ears as she sensed Tony's smiling eyes still on her. She chanced a look.

He mischievously asked, "You ready?"

"Um...I think so," she admitted, then took off the emergency brake and put the car in Drive. Tony leaned over to turn on the radio, flipping through her Bluetooth stations. One thing she was glad she had changed about this old car was the stereo. Tony stopped at one of her favorite stations as they made it to the first stop sign. "Oh, leave it there," she said.

Tony sat back, studying her.

Her heart pitched as one of her favorite indie bands began to play, and his eyes searched her for some response. He wiped his hands on the knees of his jeans and started right off the bat. "Say, you have to know, I didn't mind the kiss at all. Honestly, it was refreshing."

She blanched until the redness intensified from her chest to her ears, unable to deny her embarrassment.

Tony chuckled. "Don't be embarrassed." He reached over and took one of her hands off the steering wheel, her knuckles regaining their color.

She looked at him, then quickly back to the road. He made her far more nervous than any AP exam ever did. "I was kinda hoping you meant to kiss me. I would really like us to be more than friends."

Selah swallowed down her shock. He'd really gone right for it. "I meant it," she uttered. She sighed, letting out all her nervousness, then gave a reassuring squeeze to his hand. "Although I have to admit, I am scared. What happens if it doesn't work out? I would hate to not have you as a friend."

"It wouldn't be like that, Say. If you're not happy with me, and I pray that won't ever be the case, but if that day comes, I want you to be happy above all else." His gaze was intent as he rubbed his thumb over the soft skin of her hand. "And I will always be your friend."

She wondered if she would ever be able to stop blushing around him. She caught his sideways glance and quirked smile. "So, boyfriend, what now?" she jested.

Tony laughed. "Maybe we will have to come up with better nicknames. Boyfriend sounds so dry."

"Honey buns?"

"You like my buns?"

Her cheeks flamed again. "Maybe."

"No one can resist, I don't blame you."

"Oh, no one, huh?"

"I am irresistible what can I say?" He winked at her. "Maybe we will let the names come naturally."

She squeezed his hand again in agreement. "I like that idea."

They continued down Selah's favorite back road, the one they would usually ride down with Tony's bike. She found an open field where the cows were grazing, one where they could park and watch the sunset. The Gailton skies at dusk were always full of color and beauty.

She sensed Tony's hesitation. "What's on your mind?"

"I saw your brother last night. I'm beginning to think he is in over his head with the drugs and Quinn. His attitude is so unlike the Sean we know, it is almost scary. Last night I came very close to pummeling him," he confessed.

"Why? What happened?" She undid her seatbelt and turned to face Tony instead of the sunset. She could see his concern for Sean, which only made her worry more.

"He said some derogatory things about you, things he would have never said about you before. It's like he is becoming one of them."

She furrowed her brow in question. "What did he say?" She saw Tony's mind thinking hard, like a desperate attempt to soften the blow. "Just tell me," she interjected. "I can handle it. I know he is not my little brother right now."

"He said you were a prude, that he didn't know why I would waste my time on you."

Selah wasn't particularly shocked. She wondered the same thing, but, after all she had done for Sean, why would he say such things? The pain was deep, snagging at her heart.

She felt Tony's fingertips on her face. She hadn't realized she'd closed her eyes to fight the tears that were welling up in her eyes.

He stroked her cheek. "Say, Sean is being a fool. And fools will say crazy things, especially when under the influence of drugs and manipulation." A tear fell. Tony wiped it away, and pulled her into him, hugging her tightly.

"I am sorry, this wasn't how I envisioned tonight. Maybe tears of joy but not like this." He looked down at her giving a sympathetically playful smile. She took in a deep relieving breath.

"I know Tony, it's not your fault." She stared into his eyes trying to search for reassurance that she wasn't dreaming, but there he was solid and holding her tight. "Thank you for choosing me, and thank you for keeping an eye on my punk of a brother." More tears fell down her trembling chin. "I miss Daniel...between the two of you watching Sean I felt so much more at ease when he was out." She batted away the rest of her tears.

Tony's lips met hers. She couldn't help but melt into his kiss. He tentatively pulled away, looked deeply into her eyes. Her soul was caught under the intensity of it, as he said, "I will always choose you. And, I miss Daniel too. It still feels like a lie, him being gone. We did so much together. Feels like I lost a brother."

The rest of the evening they continued to talk. They shared childhood memories, like the time

Sean, Daniel, and Tony jumped into the creek at one of their favorite parks so they could catch frogs, only to chase Selah around with them later. Tony expressed how much he missed his parents. Selah understood, admitting how much she missed her dad too. They agreed to go to Daniel's funeral together, which seemed so sudden since it was tomorrow. Selah understood why Daniel's parents wanted to have it sooner rather than later, but it felt all too hasty for her. Grief wanted to swallow up all her joy. She felt it needling again in the back of her mind.

Suddenly, Tony perked up. "Want some happy news?" When she nodded, he went on to explain the miracle that had happened with Gramps. "It was crazy! Elle emitted this light, it was a lot like Jaidyn's, and the next thing I knew my grandpa was like totally healed. He is talking, out of bed, smiling, laughing, back to his old self. I can't quite explain how amazing it is, you will have to come see for yourself." His joy was contagious. The last time she had seen Gramps he was in a vegetative state.

"That is absolutely amazing! I will have to see him. You think he will remember me?"

Grinning, he replied, "You're pretty hard to forget, Say."

She chuckled and elbowed him. "Oh! That reminds me, um... My mom thinks we have been working out at your grandparents' in the shed." She felt ashamed for using Tony in her lies, but relief washed over her when she heard him belly laugh.

"Really? My grandparents' shed is the furthest thing from a gym, unless gyms you know have rusty garden tools and expired planting soil." He continued to laugh. Selah joined in. "I'll go along with it. I just hope your mom doesn't plan a surprise gym workout anytime soon."

She secretly prayed Elizabeth wouldn't. "I know that would kinda ruin everything. How am I supposed to tell my mom we are meeting at a church, that is now a pseudo gym, a place protected by Heaven, but to the outside world completely abandoned. Even if I gave her the name of a local gym she would likely join, and then I would really be up a creek."

"Yeah, true. I struggle to keep this life from my gram and gramps too. I hate lying to them. Though if I told them I joined a gym they would be far less likely to be bothered with joining," he chuckled. "But I still feel bad."

"Guess we will have to back each other's secrets," Selah said, snuggling in closer to Tony, then turning her gaze towards the stars. A few began to poke out from the night sky. They stayed under the cover of the stars till it was time to head back home.

Tony walked her to her front door, holding her hand. Tonight was exactly what she needed, but it continued to feel so surreal. They faced each other on her doorstep. He smiled down at her, then with his hands on her hips brought her closer to him. "I'm glad we talked."

Selah stood up on her toes, pressing her cheek to his and whispered, "Me too." Then kissed she kissed him goodnight.

●   CHAPTER 32   ●

SEAN

Sean had finished his Friday night shift and was sprawled out on his bed waiting for sleep to find him when he heard his sister come into the house. Sean knew she had been out with Tony. Some part of Sean felt weird that his longtime friend and sister were into each other. He liked Tony, no doubt, but it still felt weird. Though when Sean thought about his current relationship he wasn't in a place to say much.

Sean was gradually growing bored of his new existence—all the partying, the Doxy, and Quinn. He was beginning to care less and less about school, and anything that was once important to him. He feared that he would never get the "old Sean" back.

He missed the weekends away with his family, the times he used to spend chilling, watching stupid movies with Selah. Their relationship took a big hit when Dad died. Sean knew it was mostly his fault. He missed his sister, even when they were in the same house, just a room apart, yet he felt the many miles between them.

Every time he started thinking about the past, his mind would go back to Quinn. When did he become so obsessed? Before he took Doxy she barely knew he existed. As he lay there, staring at the ceiling, that question kept rolling around in his mind. Quinn had yet to say she loved him. Though, it didn't keep her from continuing to ask for favors, and sadly, he gave in every time. Would she do the same for him if he asked? He kinda doubted it.

A moronic idea popped into his head, Sean knew he was the craziest person to even think of such an idea, but...what if he invited Quinn to go with him to Daniel's funeral? Selah could witness Quinn being a support to Sean. It could possibly help Selah and Quinn smooth out some of their problems. He understood that Quinn was the major reason for those problems, mainly because Selah was too passive to be a threat to anyone, but this could work if he could convince Quinn to be civil.

Sean grabbed his phone off the nightstand and laid his head back on his pillow, specifying to his iPhone, "Call Quinn." The line began to ring. Sean took a steadying breath.

"Hi, Sean!"

Good, she sounds happy.

Sean continued. "Hey babe, I was wondering if you would do me a favor?"

"Sure! What is it? You want me to bring you some Doxy? A cheeseburger from Seven Guys? You name it, I can do it."

She really had no clue what he was about to ask her, or she wouldn't have said that.

"No, none of those, actually I was wondering if you would go with me to Daniel's funeral tomorrow. It would totally be cool if you could meet my mom and show some support, maybe we can smooth things out with my sister? I really like you, Quinn, and I want them to like you too."

Her hesitation was loud and clear. "Um, Sean, that is something I am really not sure I can do. Selah and I will never be friends, you realize that, right? I mean I wouldn't mind meeting your mom, but Selah and I have bad blood, and you think that a funeral is the right place for introductions and making amends?"

"Show Selah that you are a better person than she thinks you are. Also, I think my mom would be pleasantly surprised to see you supporting me like that."

"Oh, hun, I already know I am better than what Selah thinks." She laughed. "But if you really want me to be there, then I will."

"Great!" He tried not to think of all the ways this could go horribly wrong.

"I can't wait to meet your mom." She said it like she meant it. Sean felt hopeful. Now he needed to convince his sister.

"Okay babe, well, I will see you tomorrow around noon."

"Smooches."

He laughed. "Right back at ya!" And then he hung up. That went smoother than he had anticipated. It was time to go talk to Selah. He began to have second thoughts about this crazy plan, but he got up and went to his door, mustering up his best little brother smile before he could talk himself out of it. Sean knocked quietly on Selah's door. Mom was already asleep; he would wait till tomorrow to tell her.

"Come in," Selah said.

When he walked in she had a *what-do-you-want* look on her face. "What's up?"

"I had this crazy idea, and before you say no, just hear me out." He took a shaky breath. *Tread lightly Sean.* "I wanted to invite Quinn to Daniel's funeral, ya know for support."

Dropped jaw, shocked expression, disbelief. Yep, everything he expected. "Just listen, Say. I think it would be nice for Quinn to meet Mom. I know you guys don't have good ties, but maybe, just maybe, be nice for your baby brother's sake?"

She looked at him in utter annoyance.

"Sean, you are asking me to tolerate the very person that has harassed me all during high school, who wouldn't help me if I was stranded on the road to die, and of all things, during our friend's funeral!

What makes you think she would even be okay with this idea?"

Sean turned red and embarrassed. "Well, um, she already said yes." Now she really looked mad.

"The only reason she would say yes is because she can use an already difficult day, and make it even more miserable. I honestly have no idea what you see in her Sean." He felt the anger seeping into his veins.

"Listen, Sis. I want to try to have one day with my family and the girl I love."

Selah stood up, shorter than her brother, but her presence felt massive. He knew he'd pushed her too far; he could feel her radiating frustration. "You *love* her?" she said in a whispered yell as to not wake Mom. "Have you lost your damn mind, Sean? She is going to spit you out as soon as she can, you realize that, right?"

He sneered. "She is coming and that is that." His smug face pinned her anger down. He watched her temper cool as she sat back down at the head of her bed and crossed her legs. Sean followed by sitting at the foot of the bed, like they did as kids.

She shook her head, obviously aggravated at her brother's attitude. "Sean." She let out a tired groan. "I love you, but I don't think you have any idea what you're asking. She couldn't care less whether I approve of her or not. She doesn't want my respect at all or she would most certainly treat me differently." Selah looked down at her hands, wringing them before she laid them back in her lap. Sean could see the hurt that his sister often hid so well.

"Say, I am trying to be a better brother. I just want to help you and Quinn move on from the past."

Selah looked him dead in the eye, her right eyebrow raised; she looked rather skeptical.

"The other day when I saw you two together at school, she made that off-hand comment about my outfit. It's not only one incident that happened years ago, this is a continual dislike, and I don't think she cares to change. I will be civil at Daniel's funeral, but I will not sit and be ridiculed either. So, if she starts in on me, I reserve the right to stay away from her tomorrow."

Sean reached over and touched her hand, dry from turning pages in her paperback book that laid next to her. "That works for me."

She muttered as she put her other hand on top of his, "I miss you."

"I know, I miss me too."

● CHAPTER 33 ●

SELAH

Selah hid under her covers for five more minutes after her alarm sounded. She was still reeling over Sean inviting Quinn to the funeral. She was already dreading this day. Another life gone too soon, another life she couldn't save. Today they were to say goodbye to a childhood friend, her ex-boyfriend, Daniel, who was like family, and now Quinn was involved in a day that she should have had no place in.

Recent Saturdays, Selah had spent most of the day training, so when her alarm sounded again she got up and put on her workout gear, determined to let go of her frustration, guilt, and grief. She would sweat it all out, like poison. She packed her funeral attire, and almost packed her work uniform till she remembered she'd taken today off for the service. But she packed an extra change of clothes, she didn't want to come home after Daniel's service, especially if Sean and Quinn might be there with Mom.

Once she reached the church, she saw Tony's motorcycle and smiled. She was thankful that she wouldn't face this dreadful day alone. Selah got out of the car just as Jaidyn pulled into the parking lot next to her. She waited. Jaidyn hurried around the car and gave her a morning hug.

"Hey, I saw your text from late last night figured I would see you this morning. What is Sean thinking?" They linked arms and started walking.

"Seriously, I have no idea. He says he wants to help us bury the hatchet, but I am not sure he understands that shouldn't be done on the same day we are burying our friend. Nor does he understand how impossible it is for me to get along with his girlfriend."

Jaidyn couldn't comprehend it either, Selah could tell by the questioning in her eyes. "He says he likes her, that he wants us to like her too."

Jaidyn's face fell.

"I know it makes me so frustrated because he has no clue what he is doing."

Jaidyn dragged her feet a bit, musing over something Selah said. Selah couldn't figure it out, she doubted Jaidyn would either. They walked in together and saw Tony sparring with Michael. Gabriel was sullen on the couch while Uriel and Raphael warmed up on the other side of the room.

The Angels had originally planned to teach them all about what dark forces they would be fighting.

This should be interesting.

They had already learned about Luc, their fallen brother, and some of his associates. Selah worried that this new knowledge might be the beginning of some of their worst nightmares.

Michael got one last punch in. Tony dodged it. "Good job! Let's break and get on topic before workouts. Gabriel, you ready?" Michael frowned as Gabriel quietly nodded, then continued. "Today our goal is understanding how to identify the enemy. We have so far identified some of Luc's closer cohorts, like Marcus and Judas. This is why their influence on Sean is so frustrating, they seem to have their claws in pretty deep."

Selah's heart twisted.

Uriel cleared his throat to speak. "I think Luc has other plans for Sean, some important transaction. I am not sure if it is weapons or drugs at this point though. Tony and I have been trying to keep our distance from Luc as much as possible, but, with how often Sean has been in his office, it has to be something big."

Selah massaged the tension around her temples. She wanted nothing more than to shake the heck out of her brother, to wake him up before he dragged them all into this hell he'd gotten himself in.

"We will be on our guard. Tony, Uriel." Michael met each of their eyes. "Keep Sean in your sights. Let us know if anything changes or escalates. As far as other demons, here are some you may run into." He brought out pictures and paintings of various demons. At first glance one might believe they were fantasy characters or strange mythological creatures. "This one here." He pointed to an all-black figure with smooth, shiny skin like tar poured over a human form and razor-sharp bleeding teeth and claws. "This is a Shadow-Walker. They feed on fear and watch from the shadows. They do not take on human form so in that sense mortals are safe. To make them disappear one must simply change their fear to joy, like thinking of a happy memory. You can fight them, but the best way to make them freeze and bow down in submission is by calling on the name Jesus Christ. That will guarantee you the means to dispatch of them quickly. Though with other demons that are strong enough to take on human form, they will surely not leave this realm without a fight."

Selah passed around another picture, this one of a group of young maidens. One had flowing white-blond hair, with what looked like shimmering green-blue skin, and a thin, elegant form. The other one to her right had brown hair, an envious hour-glass figure, and bright pink skin. To her right, was a woman with red hair, sparkling porcelain skin, and a captivating gaze. All of them had eyes of pure onyx black, lips wrapped around sharp teeth in wicked looking smirks, and razor-sharp claws.

Michael saw her expression, "Those women in the photograph you are holding, Selah, are succubi. From what I witnessed at the club the other night, I think your brother is dating a succubus."

Selah's eyes widened. Her fingers lost their grip as she dropped the picture to the floor.

Jaidyn, who was sitting next to Selah, picked up the picture, eying it warily. She put a gentle hand on Selah's knee, instantly calming her heart.

"What does that mean?" Jaidyn asked with a mix of curiosity and determination. Selah thanked her for her resolve to ask the questions she could not.

"While it is reassuring that she hasn't influenced him to do anything significant as of yet, it makes me question how she is feeding off of him. Succubi usually seduce men, then feed on their growing lust. If things have gotten that far with Sean, then the only cure is for him to fall in love with a pure-hearted mortal, or kill the succubi in question before she kills him." He looked exhausted. "Believe me when I say that doesn't happen often. It could be the drug he is taking that keeps her influence from fully affecting him like it would most mortals. If she had full control of him, he would have been dead days ago."

Selah felt cold, all the color drained from her face. Hopelessness enveloped her. She looked at Jaidyn who gave her a sad, but hopeful smile as she rubbed her back. Selah then glanced at Tony, who had his arms crossed over his chest, determination on his face and sorrow in his eyes. He had mentioned before how he felt when he was with Anne-Marie. Could it be possible she was a succubus too? She blurted before thinking, "Could Anne-Marie be one of these, these...succubi too? She is always with Quinn and creepy as all get out."

Gabriel chimed in, "Yes, she is. I have seen her influence on a number of male students. Luckily, her influence was broken before anything fatal happened to any of them. I was able to break the bond for most of them with a good dose of truth."

She eyes fell on Tony again, thankful he wasn't under Anne-Marie's influence. "What truth did you tell them?" Selah was curious, hoping she could use the same tactic for her brother.

"I told them Anne-Marie was using them. That if they didn't get out fast she would ruin them. Like I said it didn't take much, and they aren't dead. It's safe to assume they had never been intimate with Anne-Marie." Gabriel gestured for Michael to continue. He uncovered a paper from the pile of pictures showing the hierarchy of demons and lower demons and documents citing other creatures of evil.

Selah and the others took their overwhelming thoughts back to the mat. With every kick, punch, and hit Selah made to the dummy she felt her anger leave her. She slowed her breathing and stretched the tension out of her muscles and prayed to God that she could get her brother back before it was too late.

• CHAPTER 34 •

TONY

Tony strained through each pull-up as he observed Selah beating on a defenseless sparring dummy. With every kick and jab she planted, he felt more and more inadequate to help her. The anguish and betrayal were evident on her face. He wasn't sure if it was worry over Sean, the upcoming funeral, or what she had found out about Anne-Marie, his ex, that added to her turmoil.

Uriel called him over to practice with him. They quickly got into formation, Tony leveling some even jabs when his attention went back to Selah's direction. Uriel kicked his knees out from under him, "Ey, boy-O! Where is your head?" He followed Tony's eyes and immediately understood, cocking his scarred eyebrow. "Troubles already?"

"No, no, nothing like that. Just wondering what is going on in her head. I can only imagine how overwhelmed she must feel. With all the pain today's service will bring, the constant effort of trying to keep her brother from destroying himself, all while he freely invites in evil he can't comprehend into his life and hers." Uriel helped him to his feet. "It's hard to watch her struggle with all this." He looked down at his wrapped hands. "I feel helpless. There isn't much I can do to help her."

"Sure there is!" Uriel lightly jabbed Tony's shoulder. "Fight this battle with her. We are all in this fight. Her particular struggle you may not be able to understand, but you can stand by her side."

Tony turned to Uriel, the corner of his mouth quirked up. "Thanks. Now, can you let me kick your butt?"

"Fat chance!"

They continued sparring off and on for another hour. Afterward, they each got ready for the service. Jaidyn, Selah, and Tony planned to head there together. Tony gave a short salute to Uriel as he walked out.

He met Selah by her car and gently kissed the top of her head. "You look great. Sorry it has to be for such a sad occasion." He put his arms around her neck, hugging her tight.

Jaidyn came up to the car.

"Do you want me to drive?" Tony asked Selah.

She nodded, tears already coming. He gently took her keys and ran his thumb over her hand. "I gotcha." He opened the passenger door for her, and she smiled sadly up at him. If only he could make it stop hurting. He shut the door softly.

Jaidyn was already climbing in the backseat.

Tony got in and buckled up just as Selah turned the radio on. The song "Renegades" was playing, a song each of them knew was sung by Daniel's favorite band. They looked at one another. For a moment it felt like he wasn't gone. Tony turned up the radio and drove out of the parking lot. They each sang along, tears in their eyes. Daniel was forever with them.

When they arrived at the chapel next to the graveyard, Tony parked. Selah gazed at him with those deep seas of cerulean speckled with gold, and as she leaned over, her lips brushed his. "Thank you for always being there for me when I need you most...both of you." She looked back to Jaidyn. "I don't know if I am ready for this, or to see Quinn, but I know I have to." He gently squeezed her hand as Jaidyn touched her shoulder. Selah took a steadying breath. "Okay, let's do this."

Jaidyn quickly got out the back.

Tony held Selah back for a second. "Say." He touched her face, still pink and damp from crying. "You say the word, and we will leave. I promise." She leaned in, kissed him again. He could taste the salt from her tears, though her lips were warm and gentle. Sobriety had nothing on what he felt right now. Selah was the sun and he the moon. He would shine for her, when she could no longer shine herself.

"Just help me watch after Sean, that is far more than enough." She smiled, wiping away the dampness from her face. She was radiant, even in her pain.

"I will." It was a promise he intended to keep. If not for Sean, then his desire to help Selah solidified his decision.

"Thank you." She opened her door and stood next to Jaidyn. They held on to each other as Tony rounded the car. They began to walk, Tony following behind them. Selah wore a simple pantsuit while Jaidyn wore a black bohemian style dress; both of them looked beautiful despite the melancholy black.

They were greeted by familiar faces, all solemn, especially Daniel's parents. There was no viewing. Apparently, rumor had it, Daniel's body was still in the morgue. Tony was reminded of his parent's funeral. They were in the morgue during their memorial too. It was for the best. The last thing he would have wanted to see was the bodies of his parents, inanimate and lifeless. At least this way he could still look back on their smiles and remember the warmth of his mother's hugs. It saddened his heart to count four lives lost already in their tight-knit group of friends. Selah's dad, his parents, and now Daniel. They really need to help Sean before he became the next one in the morgue.

For the remainder of the service people spoke of Daniel's kindness, courage, and athleticism. His parents reminded everyone that tomorrow isn't promised, that Daniel was a great example of taking every day as it came. Their only grief was over the promising future he could have had and that they must wait to see him again.

Selah was a puddle of tears. Tony reached over to draw her in close. Sean sat next to Jaidyn and Quinn on his other side. Tony caught his eye. Sean gripped Quinn's hand, silent tears streaming down his clenched jawline. Sean looked at Jaidyn, sobbing too, and shoulder hugged her with his other arm. Selah's mom, Elizabeth, was sitting near Daniel's parents, trying to be a comfort to them. All they had left was each other. He vowed that this family wouldn't dwindle any more than it already had.

Set-up right after the service was a small reception where friends and family of Daniel's could converse and share their memories of him. Their little group sat together. Quinn had just excused herself to the bathroom when the rest of them sat down. When she came back Tony caught her furious expression as she saw Jaidyn and Sean talking. Selah had gone to give Daniel's mom a hug.

"This is one sorry group. Funerals always make me feel icky," Quinn said with a squirm.

"Wow, Quinn, have some respect for the dead, will ya." Tony said.

Sean defended her. "No, I get it. I feel caged up right now, all this crying and sadness just hurts."

Quinn raised a brow. Tony was sure that wasn't at all what she meant. He wondered if succubi also sucked the joy and compassion out of their victims' lives.

Selah sat down, a mournful smile on her face. "His mom is holding up so well, considering. This whole thing is so incredibly tragic."

"That outfit is tragic," Quinn mumbled.

Selah looked plainly at Sean. "Really?"

"Quinn, please. Be kind, for me," Sean pleaded.

"Fine." She sighed and put her elbows on the table and leaned in. "What if I told you I know a place where we can forget about all this sadness for a bit?"

Sean was curious. "Where?"

"There is a haunted house set up for Halloween next week. It's in one of the vacant fields outside of town. I can get us in for free. My parents own the field and know the owners of the company that put on the haunted houses." Quinn looked rather enthusiastic about the prospect.

Selah on the other hand glared at her with skepticism.

"Come on Say, doesn't it sound like fun? Something to get our minds off all this craziness that has been going on."

Tony raised a brow. He wasn't sure if Sean understood he was most of the reason for the recent "craziness" going on.

Selah locked eyes with Jaidyn, who gave a gentle, approving nod. Tony was sure this meant she wouldn't leave Selah with them alone. It was decided, they were all going.

"Great! Meet me at this address." Quinn pulled out a few flyers from her clutch, handing one to each of them. The flyer showed a grotesque image of a clown, inviting everyone with bold letters to:

Inferno: The Fair of Horrors and Enchantments.

"It opens at seven." Quinn grinned at Sean, who smiled back reassuringly.

Tony wasn't quite so reassured.

After the reception, they each said their goodbyes. Sean left with Quinn. Tony drove the girls back to the church. "Say, you sure you're okay with going to this thing tonight? It's okay to say no, we could make up some reason not to go." Tony feared they were walking into something they couldn't walk away from.

"Sean will go without us. Someone needs to be there." She caught his eyes as Tony glanced her way. "I can't let him end up like Daniel."

That settled it then. "Okay, then we all go." He looked in the rearview mirror at Jaidyn.

She answered, "That's right." Something about her expression looked faraway, but Tony knew she was in this with her best friend till the end.

•   CHAPTER 35   •

GABRIEL

The Angels watched Daniel's memorial from afar while the Chosen were at the reception. Gabriel felt he needed to pay his respects, though nothing would take away the overwhelming guilt that weighed on his soul. The Angels, even Archangels, were not infallible; they made mistakes, but when failure happened it hit hard. Gabriel knew that Uriel grieved over "the Fall of Man" and how Lucifer bypassed his watch. Michael still felt responsible for Lucifer's own shortcomings and having to send him to Hell. Raphael was unable to heal everyone. These losses, they stacked up, one after the other, and after eons of time, they began to feel insurmountable.

They had come back to Raph's apartment after the service. Gabriel sat on the couch, his elbows on his knees, his head downcast, and hands in his hair.

Michael and Uriel sat on either side in the armchairs.

Raph called over her shoulder as she shuffled around in the kitchen, "Tea is always helpful. I will put a pot on."

Michael spoke sincerely, "Brother, I am sorry you're going through this pain. It is overwhelming, I know."

"I wasn't prepared for it to make me feel so helpless. I should have stepped in long before we did. Daniel could still be here, if we weren't more concerned about their shock from what they would learn. We could have just told them, let the shock set in and move on," Gabriel bargained with himself.

Uriel said, "This game of what-if will be hard to get out of, Gabe. Sadly, what has happened, happened, and we cannot undo it. All we can do now is learn from it. Daniel is in Heaven. That fact is what we have to hold onto as we help the Chosen who are still here."

Gabriel groaned and leaned back on the couch, staring at the ceiling. "Father, help us. I don't think I can take another failure right now."

Raphael put a comforting hand on his shoulder as she handed him a hot cup of tea.

"He will see us through it all, Brother."

Uriel's phone rang.

"Boy-O, what is going on?" They all knew it was Tony on the other end. "Oh, that's strange. She must be up to something. Be cautious. Wait, where is this place?"

He listened to Tony, then replied, "She is definitely up to something. That address is for the Inferno. There is a conduit on that land that leads to Hell. That's why it has remained vacant for so long." Uriel looked at his brother and sister as he continued. "When are you guys headed there?" He waited for an answer. "Okay, don't go in till you see me or one of the other's pull up there. Delay Sean if you can." Tony agreed and hung up.

Uriel rubbed the back of his neck. "That succubus, the one with Sean, invited the Chosen to a haunted house. It apparently is on one of Hell's ley lines."

Gabriel sat up straight with his cup in both hands. "We won't let them in there alone."

Michael interrupted, "We can't go into a conduit. We can follow them. Pray for them, and equip them. But we can't infiltrate Hell, or go near its gateways, or believe me that would have happened eons ago."

Gabriel knew this, but he wasn't about to let them go in blindly. "Uriel call Tony back, tell him to stay at the church, we are going over there now." He stared pointedly at Michael. "We are equipping them tonight. They have to have a means to protect themselves if we can't protect them."

Michael nodded.

It was time to give the Chosen their weapons, and the Angels only had a few hours to prep them, but Gabriel was determined to not let this opportunity pass by. Raph grabbed her keys and said, "I'll drive."

Michael and Uriel stood next to a table full of swords, daggers, and other handheld weapons. On Uriel's other side stood Raphael. Next to her was a rack filled with bows, crossbows with their corresponding arrows, and a row of short staffs. On the opposite side of the church Gabriel was at the ready. The case next to him displayed long staffs, whips, and flails.

Selah's heart jumped in nervous excitement. It brought no joy knowing she would have to carry such weapons, but at least now she was physically able to wield such defensive weapon. She glanced at Tony with his fierce demeanor, then over to Jaidyn. Her face held a sadness, but her solid stance reassured Selah that they were as ready as she was.

Michael stepped forward and commanded, "Look around. Feel the weapons. Hold on to the ones that make your heart race. Your weapon will be an extension of God's will and your purpose. Choosing your weapon is a spiritual experience. It can feel a bit overwhelming at first, but once your weapon finds you then we will begin.

Selah headed straight for two short swords—sharp, double-edged swords, each a twin of the other. The pummel design consisted of intricate swirls surrounding the Star of David. On the guard were more swirls etched into the steel, running halfway down each blade. They were beautiful. Selah moved her hand off the leather-wrapped handle, where she spotted an embroidered golden cross. She sparred with an invisible foe, dancing with the blades. She smiled, knowing she'd found her match in seconds.

Michael quirked a smile as he watched Selah continue sparring with her short swords. It had always been blades for Michael. He owned the Soul Sword, which flamed with God's Judgment as he pulled it out to spar with her. He got in fighting stance when he said, "Your blades are known as the Blades of Jonathan, Armor Bearer to King David. Precise and lethal." He moved to take a jab, and the clang of metal rang through the room.

Jaidyn walked over to Raphael, a bit frazzled. She asked, "How am I to pick a weapon when my purpose is to heal?" Raph put her hand gently on

Jaidyn's shoulder, explaining the difference between harming demons and humans. "Angels, and now you, the Chosen, are entrusted to protect humanity. Meaning we are tasked with sending demons and their kind back to the Hell, where they belong."

Jaidyn nodded, understanding. She picked up a staff of glowing gold fortified by lightweight titanium.

"The Savior's Scepter." Raphael breathed in awe. The staff was light, Jaidyn twirled and brandished it, her body and the staff a hypnotic combo that would likely render an opponent dizzy before the first blow. Her graceful form was a perfect mirror of such an elegant weapon. Jaidyn finished and tapped the bottom end of the staff on the ground to rest, and two lethal wings made of curved knives popped out right under the pommel of the staff. Jaidyn's eyes widened.

She heard Selah stop sparring. Jaidyn looked to her friend as she chuckled. "It really is like you, Jay, refined and elegant until provoked."

Even the deadly pummel was beautiful, a crown of thorns wrapped around a flaming heart.

Exquisite, till I hit someone with it. Jaidyn gulped.

"It also compacts into a smaller scepter." Raphael tapped it again against the ground and the wings retracted, then she pressed a button in the middle of the jeweled heart, and the lower parts of the staff slid smoothly up to reveal only a couple feet of metal and the pummel. "If you do not retract the wings though it can be used as a mace."

Jaidyn grasped it tentatively as Raph handed her the weapon. "Understood."

Jaidyn nodded.

At last they gathered quietly as Tony continued to search for his soul's mated instrument. He closed his eyes; he whispered a prayer. Uriel stood near his table as Gabriel walked over to him. "You okay? What's holding you back?"

"Honestly, I don't have a clue," he beseeched Uriel and Gabriel. "All I keep thinking is, I am not good enough to use any of these weapons. I am just a mechanic and a sober bartender. How can we...I mean,

I, defeat any of these demons?" Tony peered down at his hands, and all he saw were the calluses and grime, and still no weapon.

Uriel then walked over, put his hands on both of Tony's shoulders, looked him in the eye then spoke directly to his soul. "Don't for one second think you are not worthy of the call, boy. God has chosen you and your friends to help us defeat evil, and we need you to do precisely that. The only way you could let us down is if you continue to doubt what God has ordained. I promise you He will see you through—you only have to be willing to take on the call."

Tony's shoulders straightened. He stood taller with each word spoken unto him. He lifted his chin with a smile.

Each of the Chosen stood much the same way when Uriel was done.

Tony stepped back, glancing at his choices once again. So many marvelous weapons. He began meandering around the tables and cases and froze mid-step at the table Michael and Uriel had originally been stationed at. He gripped a short, nondescript sword. It looked Roman made. He fingered the leather armor of a wrist mounted crossbow. Next to it laid a black leather belt sheathing almost a dozen short steel cross engraved arrows.

Uriel came up behind him with a toothy grin. "The Sword of Peter, and the crossbow was once mine, before I was given the Guardian Sword of Eden. I know you will use both well and wisely." Uriel proudly clapped his hand on Tony's shoulder and with a bellowing call to all of them, he said, "Now, time to practice before you leave tonight."

Eyeing their funeral attire, Raphael spoke up. "That reminds me." She pointed to a table stacked with what looked to be stealth combat gear. Black cargo pants in their sizes, varying colors of form-fitted short-sleeve tops with what felt like moisture wicking. "These clothes can be worn anywhere. The tops have built-in bullet proof armor that can only be seen with a spiritual eye. This battle gear is made for occasions such as tonight, when you're unsure of your safety and know you may be heading into something dangerous. For all other times if you just wear one of the tops under your regular clothes it will still leave you protected, for the most part."

They picked through the pile and got a few outfits each, then went to change. When they came out,

Tony wore all black, his crossbow strapped to his wrist and short sword sheathed diagonally across his back for easy unsheathing.

Jaidyn had a sage-green top with her black cargo pants, and her mace staff was in her hand." Raphael squeaked, "Oh my gosh, that's right!" She walked over to Jaidyn, taking the mace from her hand, and twisted the crown of thorns. The whole thing shrank to a winged pendant, which dangled from a golden chain. "This beauty was retrofitted to become nearly undetectable." She smiled as she handed it back to Jaidyn. "Just push the jewel again and it will return to a mace, then one more time for the full staff."

Jaidyn's smile glowed with the rest of her.

Selah gave a cursory smile. She stood resolute in her black pants and magenta top, as Michael helped her buckle her double sheath for her short swords around her shoulders. The blades fit, handles out, resting on each side of where her waist met her hips. The sheath rested in the middle of her lower back. All she would have to do is reach back and pull them out. She and Tony could easily hide their weapons with a good jacket.

They practiced maneuver after maneuver, defensive and offensive tactics. Michael spoke over the grunts, kicks, and jabs. "Remember the weapons you wield are an extension of yourself, of your own powers. When you glow, it is easier to transfer your power to your weapon. It will also take less energy for you to defeat your adversary."

Selah felt him beside her. "Concentrate on awakening the glow, the light of God inside you. With every motion let that glow seep into the blades." He directed at Selah, but referred to each of them. "Let your power flow like oil over your weapon."

Each of them moved toward their imaginary targets and in spectacular show, each of their weapons began to glow. Tony's sword burned with bright-red flames, Jaidyn's staff radiated a glorious lavender light, and the swirls in Selah's blades lit up brightly with her golden light.

They each looked confident, ready, strong, but they still had an unnerving night ahead of them.

•   C H A P T E R   3 6   •

URIEL

As the Chosen finished up and headed out the door, Uriel's heart started beating erratically. He headed to the couch in the common area to sit. His hands began to tremble. Uriel felt that familiar comforting warmth and immediately shut his eyes. He knew what was coming next. God was relaying a message, usually in the form of visions or a dream, but once Uriel felt his Father's call he shut out every distraction around him.

As if far away, he could hear Michael ask what was wrong. Gabriel quickly understood what was happening, being a messenger himself, and informed Michael.

Raphael held Uriel's right hand to be a conduit of comfort, Gabriel took his left to be his strength and a witness to what God was about to reveal.

Uriel's spirit awoke in a field, the "Inferno: House of Horrors and Enchantments" sign lit up near a ramshackle carnival with a haunted house looming in the back. He overheard Tony and Sean as they walked into the major haunted house exhibits.

"Sean, what is it you need to get for Luc?"

"I don't know. All I know is if I don't my family is in trouble." Both of them disappeared in a cloak of black smoke, and Uriel was teleported to a dark room.

This room was big, like their gutted-out church, but this warehouse was industrial, filled with various tools scattered about, and burners underneath beakers of all shapes and sizes, while pills and the dust of various drugs covered rows of tables.

He looked around, hearing a voice from another room. His mind followed the voice. When he came into the room no one batted an eye; he knew they could not see him. As he stepped closer to the subjects, he could make out the snarl of his brother Lucifer, his face full of hate, and next to him were two towers of pure muscle and no brains, a couple of his lackeys. They glared at a woman strapped to a chair.

"You can squirm all you want but unless Sean comes back with my package, you will be seeing Jesus a lot sooner than you intended." He wore that vain, wicked smirk like he'd said something amusing, making Uriel want to knock his teeth in. Uriel gritted his teeth and continued to listen.

"Where are Sean and Selah?" Elizabeth gasped. It was her voice that made Uriel turn around to see her face. What was Lucifer playing at? Uriel looked at his fallen brother, but a whirlwind of light blinded him.

He flashed into another agonizing moment of helplessness. Uriel saw Sean screaming next to his sister's crumpled body. A growl escaped Sean as he yelled at Lucifer, "You promised they wouldn't get hurt!"

"As I recall it wasn't me who promised you that..." His voice trailed off before Uriel could determine where Elizabeth was, though they were still in the warehouse. Uriel was surrounded by waves of light when he heard God speak, "Here lies the turning point for the Chosen."

The warmth began to dissipate like fog gone adrift. Uriel shivered. His senses slammed back into the here and now. He let out a gasp as he opened his eyes in shock.

Gabriel let out a breath he seemed to have been holding the whole time, and Raphael looked worn.

"What did you see?" Michael asked.

Uriel shook his head, trying to shake out the wisps of lingering grogginess. "From what I can gather, Lucifer is having Sean pick up a package at Inferno. Tony was with him. Elizabeth was also being held as a hostage." He said as more of a question than a statement, "When Sean delivers Luc's package, Selah is already dead?" He looked to Gabriel to confirm. "Right?"

Gabriel nodded grimly. "Yes, that was what I witnessed."

Raphael wrung her hands.

Michael got up and started pacing. "When is this supposed to happen?"

Uriel rubbed his knees, trying to rid his hands of nervous sweat. He looked up to catch Michael's worried gaze. "I would assume tonight since the Chosen are heading to the Inferno as we speak. But the Inferno is definitely not the warehouse I saw in the last part of the vision. Maybe this warehouse is where Sean will be dropping off whatever he is retrieving?" Uriel looked to Michael for hope.

"Then who do we follow tonight?" Raphael asked with concern. "Sean and one of our own, who are about to step foot into the gates of Hell, or Elizabeth, who could be abducted while we are following Tony and Sean?"

Michael's brows furrowed. "Well...we do the logical thing and split up. But, Uriel, if you have any clearer visions keep us in the loop.

Uriel nodded and added, "God wanted us aware of the coming scenario, though He also stated tonight was a changing point for the Chosen— something about tonight is meant to happen."

Michael added, "Then we pray that God will guide us in our purpose and position in this battle." Uriel saw Michael square his shoulders likely to reassure himself, but all Uriel could feel was the weight of his human form and the unknown ahead. Life seemed so much easier when he was just an Archangel, mowing down demons and sending them to the underworld. The weight of humanity, of making the right decision for all those involved was a new sensation he wasn't sure he liked. He would never envy God, because only the Lord Almighty could carefully bob and weave through these issues throughout eternity.

Michael witnessed the unsteadiness in Uriel. He understood the pressure to try to make the best and right decision, especially after a vision like that. Being chief Archangel was more than enough responsibility. He looked encouragingly to his second in command, Raphael.

Raphael looked back at Michael and said, "My suggestion is that you and I stay with Elizabeth, Gabriel and Uriel should follow the Chosen like we planned."

They continued to talk about strategy, how they would communicate, and plan for the worst-case scenario. They decided through much deliberation that they would stick to Raphael's assigned groups, and they would use radio types of devices in their ears to communicate. Gabriel had already purchased them right after the incident with Daniel at the club. The inconvenient part about not revealing their full nature to humanity, was that they could no longer utilize their communication abilities where they could telepathically inform one another of what was happening. Before they could travel across the Earth and still communicate clearly. This world's way of communication would have to make due.

They changed into their own battle gear, tested their radios, then prayed. They prayed that tonight they wouldn't fail the Chosen, that they could change the outcome of this night, and that God would lead the way.

• CHAPTER 37 •

LUCIFER

Quinn put down her phone and turned to face Luc. "This is going to be like stealing candy from a baby." Her face lit up with a wicked smirk as she tiptoed her sharp black finger nails up Luc's chest. She slipped her hand underneath his shirt collar and around his neck.

He let her pull him into a deep kiss. Luc mumbled a laugh into her kiss. "You're a cold-hearted snake Quinathra." He pulled her in deeper to the dark recesses of their booth. "What did you work out for my plan?"

She raked her nails through his hair. "Sean's mom will be at home alone tonight as I take the younglings to Inferno. That should give you the perfect opportunity to get what you need." She smiled against his lips. Her desire to be the queen of the underworld was far too strong, making it all too easy to use her to get to Selah.

"Good girl."

Selah and her brother had no idea what they were walking into tonight. Luc needed this transaction to run as smoothly as possible, and if he could kill a Chosen one in the process, then this could work out better than he hoped. With Quinathra convincing Sean and the others to go, Luc could now kill another one of the Chosen and find once and for all if the others were blessed with these powers.

Luc grinned from ear to ear. He didn't need hope, just well-placed manipulation. He would get those unholy weapons, even if he had to burn through tons of human drudges to do so. With Doxy working better than he had planned on quite a few subjects, he had a small handful of subjects to choose from, but Sean was definitely their most promising lab rat.

Luc would capture their mother, giving Sean more incentive to get the job done right. Sean must come back with the shipment intact and alive, which would be preferable, but not necessary.

He shoved Quinn off of him. She giggled like a crazed schoolgirl. Luc stood up, straightening his navy-blue suit vest and white dress shirt. He brushed off his navy dress slacks and left Quinn there giggling as she continued to drink from a cup of Luc's intoxicating blood; a payment he was willing to make for her help. He didn't look back as he grabbed his suit jacket. He exited the club and left in his usual limo. "To the warehouse," he said.

When he arrived at the warehouse, he called on two of his most average-looking guards, though their average looks did not keep them from being supernaturally lethal. "Shut the door behind you." Luc barked. "Tonight, both of you will head to this address." He handed over a slip of paper. "And you will kidnap this woman." He slammed a picture of Elizabeth Moore down on top of the paper. "Be discreet. We don't need the cops involved. Then bring her straight here. Understood?"

They both affirmed, "Yes, sir."

"And send two lieutenants to Inferno to follow Quinathra with the Chosen One and her friends.

Quinn will send Sean to retrieve my weapons, and I want to be assured those weapons arrive without issue. Sean should bring them to me, but if he can't make it to the warehouse, your men will make sure those weapons get here." He smiled viciously as both the men nodded. All his men knew Sean, so he didn't bother reminding them of his face. "And if they happen to see any meddling Angels be sure they do not get their hands on my shipment!"

The men stood straighter. They were aware of what would happen if they failed. He waved the men off. "Carry on.

"Okay, hun, Sean told me already." She grinned, knowing Selah and Sean would finally be spending some time together. "Have fun with your brother, keep him outta trouble." Elizabeth yawned. "I will likely be in bed when you get home, but don't stay out too late. Love you."

She tapped the screen, hanging up the call, and picked the TV remote back up. With all her recent overtime, a funeral, and constant worry over the kids, her brain needed a break. A Netflix binge was definitely in order.

She took the remote with her to the kitchen, skimming through options as she made some hot chocolate. She had already changed into her pajamas the moment she left the funeral, not planning to go anywhere else tonight.

It grieved her heart to think of Daniel, such a sweet young man, now gone. She thought of Sean and Selah. What on earth would she do if either one of them were to die before her? She couldn't think of it without her heart hitching a beat and a deep desire to cry. Her heart broke when she lost Dean—but not her kids. Never her kids.

Elizabeth stopped her mind from thinking such depressing thoughts and made her way back to the couch. She grabbed a yummy, fuzzy blanket on the couch arm and snuggled it as she sipped her warm cocoa. She needed laughs, lots of them. She picked *Nacho Libre*, one of their family's favorite movies.

She shot up off the couch, dropping her blanket the moment she heard the handle on the front door jiggle. Selah wasn't coming home, and Sean had just left to meet up with Quinn. She went to her purse on the entry table to grab her taser, but before she could reach it the door slammed inward. Two overly muscled men grabbed her. One quickly covered her mouth with an overly fragrant cloth as she flailed, trying to keep them from grabbing her legs and arms. It was too late. Her eyes fluttered as the blackness closed in.

CHAPTER 38

SEAN

Sean walked into AfterBurn and spotted Quinn. He could tell she had already had her fill of refreshments. He rubbed his eyes with the heel of both hands, trying to get his eyes to adjust to the room. Quinn was giddy, he didn't mind that. Most days she was pretty tightly wound, it was a nice change. He smiled as she ran up to him and wrapped her arms around him. She kissed him then took his hand, walking him over to the booth in the back, not their normal VIP booth, but a darker, more private booth. Her mouth was rimmed with red as she smiled at him and she sat down. He slid in beside her. On the table laid out for the ready were a few doses of Doxy. "For you," she said.

Sean couldn't say no. He took it willingly.

"What's gotten into you?" he asked as he sat back up, feeling the drug dissolve down the back of his throat. He sniffed, then gazed into her eyes; they were strangely full and expectant.

"Just excited to show you that I can get along with your sister. In fact, tonight I kinda need you to do something. Luc needs a shipment to be picked up at Inferno. It's being held at the haunted houses. And I thought while you did that I could escort the others around the park. Inferno is like a scary theme park, so there are tons of food spots and things to see— though you will probably need Tony's help, the boxes Luc needs are pretty heavy," She rambled on.

Sean tilted his head. "You want to escort my sister and Jaidyn alone?" He knew Selah wasn't going to be thrilled about splitting up, but if Quinn was trying to be better then he needed to give her this chance to do so. "Okay, good luck." He paused, dusting off the table. "Do you happen to know what exactly I am picking up?"

"No, just that it is heavy. Probably some rare liquor or something for the bar. You know Luc likes to pinch his pennies and cut corners." She didn't sound convincing, but he didn't really care.

The Doxy hit his entire system now, energizing him from head to toe. Sean grabbed Quinn and kissed her hard. "I'm ready when you are, babe."

Selah stood by her car, arms crossed over her chest, waiting for her brother and Quinn to come out of AfterBurn so they could follow them to this place that would apparently help her forget her grief. She wasn't ready to make friends with Quinn, that much she was sure of. But with Tony and Jaidyn here with her, she promised herself she would try to have a good time. Tony had his arm around her waist, standing next to her. He pulled her closer, making her feel more solid. Jaidyn cleaned underneath her nails as she stood on the other side of her. Selah asked, "Do we really have to do this?"

Tony replied, "We aren't even sure what we are walking into really. It could be as innocent as Quinn makes it out to be, or we could very well be using our newly learned skills tonight." He seemed excited about that possibility. "At least our weapons aren't noticeable and we can hopefully smuggle them in with us." He tugged on her leather jacket and grinned.

"Yeah, I know. I can't get over this uneasy feeling I have, though whenever my brother or Quinn are involved. That uneasy feel is apparent. Lately, I have felt it more often, even without them around, like something is about to happen and I can't stop it."

Jaidyn turned to look at her. "Say, no matter what we are here. We will walk through whatever comes together, and we will drag Sean with us if we have to."

Selah smiled at the thought of Sean kicking and screaming as they dragged him. "I know." She let go of Tony to hug her tight. As they pulled away from each other Sean and Quinn came prancing out of the club. Selah frowned. She could tell Sean was high. *Great!* She glared at Quinn.

"What?" Quinn questioned, then laughed absently. "Y'all ready for a good time?"

"Looks like you started without us," Tony scoffed.

Selah tried to hide her smirk as he continued. "We're ready. We will follow you guys there." He winked at Selah as he went to her driver side to drive again. Selah turned, opened her door, and got in on the passenger side.

Sean blurted, "Jay, you wanna come with us?"

Jaidyn went pallid. "Um..." She looked to Selah.

Selah nodded.

"Sure, that's fine."

Selah gave a grateful smile to her friend. What would she do without her constant companionship? She was grateful Jaidyn would be in the car because that meant that Sean would be far more careful. Even though it was Quinn's car he was driving.

Then Jaidyn got brave. "Why don't I drive?" She looked at Quinn. "Would that be okay?"

Quinn smiled sinfully. "Sure, Sean and I can sit in the back together. Great idea."

Jaidyn rolled her eyes as Quinn headed toward her back seat.

Selah mouthed to Jaidyn, "I'm sorry."

"You owe me," she mouthed back.

CHAPTER 39

SELAH

As Tony followed Jaidyn in Quinn's silver Mercedes, Selah's mind traveled over the possibilities of what they might face. Would they even recognize a demon if they saw one? She remembered something Michael had told her. "The Spirit will tell you." Sure, she had learned about the Holy Spirit when she was in Sunday school, but she couldn't recall the last time she actually was directed by it.

"Tony, have you ever heard the Holy Spirit?" She glanced at him with a questioning gaze.

His lips formed an easy smile. "Honestly, the only time I can remember is with my parents, the night of the crash. I sensed something wasn't right. A dreaded feeling, so strong I felt it to my core. However, the only other time I have felt that way was when I was thinking about dating Anne-Marie. So, I am not quite sure if the last time was the Holy Spirit or not."

Selah sighed. "I'm worried we will walk into this place tonight and not be able to differentiate demon from mortal. I feel comfortable vanquishing demons but killing a mortal..." She paused. "I just don't want to make any mistakes."

He reached over with a free hand and squeezed her knee. "Say, we know we have to protect each other and Sean. Everything else we will face as it comes. I can assume if our weapons hurt a mortal then they will stop fighting in fear of being harmed; while a demon, I would assume, wouldn't let up till they were dead." He tilted his head in thought. "Do they die?"

"See, that's what I mean. We were so caught up in practice and maneuvers, I think we should have asked some questions." She laughed tensely.

"Well, whatever happens, we do it together. The angels wouldn't have sent us into this fight if we weren't ready."

"True." She felt reassured by her twin blades pressed against the small of her back. She fiddled with the cuff of her leather jacket. "I guess I am just worried. I see Quinn, and I know what she truly is, but she looks so innately human, it's uncanny really. How are we to know the difference with others we see?"

He nodded in agreement. "I see your point, but we must fight whatever or whomever attacks Sean or us. In the end, it doesn't quite matter what they are."

Tony gave her another tempered grin. "God knows the heart, Say, so don't worry." He squeezed her leg once more before he had to use both hands to turn.

Selah saw the neon flashing sign up ahead. "Inferno" blared brightly against the night sky. Her chest tightened, but she refused to walk in fear. Selah said a silent prayer and gathered her courage.

"No matter what, we got each other's back. You ready?" Tony inquired as he parked Selah's car next to Quinn's.

"As ready as I'll ever be." Her courage fell flat at the end of that statement.

Tony unbuckled, turned to face her, and grabbed her hand. "I don't do this often, so bear with me." He closed his eyes. "Lord, we ask you to give us courage, strength, and guidance. Do not let fear be our guide, only your will and might. In Jesus's name, amen."

Immediately, Selah felt a resolve she didn't have before. "Thank you," she breathed and then gave him a quick kiss. "Let's kick some demon butt!"

Jaidyn and the others were already out of Quinn's car when Selah opened her door. Tony approached from the other side.

Jaidyn looked angry, not a look Selah saw often on her face, but when she saw Quinn and Sean were still sucking face outside of the car, she understood why. Jaidyn gave a scathing glance toward Quinn, then an exhausted one to Selah. "Come on." Selah grabbed her arm and locked elbows with hers as they started toward the entrance.

"They were like that the whole drive here," Jaidyn informed her.

"I'm sorry." Selah was. This was not fair to her friend. Selah had seen the recent concern in Jaidyn for Sean. She guessed that her feelings were deeper than friendly. Selah believed her best friend deserved far better than her brother. She was hopeful that one day soon he would break from that monster's hold and see what he was missing out on. Selah wished that tonight that spell he was under would be broken.

One could hope.

She hugged her friends arm as they continued to walk. They stopped at the end of the line. This place was unusually busy for such a small town like Gailton. Though, much like AfterBurn, when there isn't much to choose from for entertainment, you take what you can get.

"Why is there a line?" Tony wondered out loud. "I thought this was a free venue."

"It is, for us. But like most places everyone who comes in has to be stamped and checked for safety," Quinn said with a grin.

Does she know we are armed?

Tony stepped closer to Selah and whispered, "Um...hopefully they don't do a pat down."

Both Jaidyn and Selah tensed.

Selah tried impossibly to relax. She realized the guiltier she looked the more likely it would be that security would check.

"Act innocent," she murmured to the two of them.

To their luck, there were no metal detectors. Their feigned innocence and nonchalance must have worked because they squeaked in without a second glance.

Quinn flirted with the ticket booth guys. "Hi, fellas, we are to get in free." The guy rolled his eyes, as if he already knew who she was. He likely did.

"The stamp will allow you into any of the attractions, but there are no in-and-out privileges," droned the uncaring attendant as he stamped all their hands.

"Well, that was close." Tony let out an exasperated sigh once they were on the other side of the entrance.

"I told you I had it covered," Quinn said, not knowing to what Tony was referring to.

Tony arrogantly smiled. "Thanks."

Selah tried not to laugh.

"Don't thank me quite yet. Sean needs to pick up something for Luc tonight, so I kinda need you to help him. We can split up in about an hour, since we will have to leave when you're done. This way we can enjoy some thrills before we have to go." She had the whole night figured out.

As they walked down the main thoroughfare they were bombarded by a display of grotesque horrors. A man withered to the bone was trying to sell popcorn to passersby. On the other side were games of nightmarish proportions— "Smashing Skulls." The purpose of this particular game was to knock down skulls that popped up at you. The sickening crunch that came from the game when the skulls were hit with the mallet made Selah's stomach turn. She wondered if they were actual human skulls.

She huddled closer to Jaidyn as they continued down the path. Severed heads on stakes were mounted at one booth, waiting for players to toss rings around their heads, while blood and gore oozed down the metal poles they were attached to.

Jaidyn's pallor took on an ash color.

Tony's jaw was clenched as he walked protectively next to Selah and Jaidyn. Selah was sure he caught her shocked expression when he asked, "This can't be real."

Quinn squealed, "Oh, let's get our fortune told!"

Sean grimaced but followed her into a garish gypsy style tent.

Selah, Jaidyn, and Tony slid cautiously into the tent behind them. As they entered Selah noticed the burnt black licorice smell, the ghoulish green lights bouncing off the tent's fabric walls, and in the middle of the smoke-filled room was a small round table with only two chairs. Quinn quickly sat Sean down in the seat as a woman came quietly out of a curtained off area.

"Hello, mortals." She smiled a dirty rotten smile and sat with some fanfare across from Sean. "Good evening. Would you like me to tell your fortune?"

"Sure," Sean groaned unenthusiastically.

Quinn swatted his back. "Oh, come on, Sean, it will be fun." She looked to the scary woman. "You'll see." She nodded to her. "Go on."

The woman pulled a scarf off the table to reveal a crystal ball. She stared into the orb as the lights in the tent began to flicker. Selah glanced around as the woman croaked. "Oh."

Sean glared into the orb. "What? What do you see?"

"Oh, my boy, you have a winding road ahead of you." Her brows lifted in surprise. "But good things will come if you follow the heart."

Sean rolled his eyes at that.

"Okay, my turn." Quinn sat on Sean's lap as the woman cleared her mind with the use of jazz fingers and unholy groaning. Selah bit the inside of her cheek. This was ridiculous.

"Darkness!" the woman blurted. "All I see is darkness. Your future looks rather bleak my dear." She looked more entertained than concerned for Quinn. Maybe she knew who and what she was.

•   CHAPTER 40   •

SELAH

Quinn stomped out of the fortune teller's tent in a huff. "What does she know? She has no idea who she is talking to. I will have her fired."

Selah shook her head.

Jaidyn pursed her lips.

"I thought it was funny. Who believes these people anyway?" Sean chuckled as he headed toward a vendor who was dressed impressively as a zombie. Sean threw down a dollar in the zombie's box and grabbed one of the pretzels. The zombie man gave a thankful groan. "Let's go to the theatre." He pointed at a ramshackle sign, where severed hands pointed in the direction of different amusements.

"Gruesome," Jaidyn observed.

The sign to the theatre could be read from where they stood. It stated they were about to show a rendition of *Dante's Inferno*.

"Actually, can we go on the Ferris wheel before we split up? Not really in the mood to watch a story about Hell," Tony objected.

Selah understood. It already felt like they had the odds stacked against them without being reminded of the evils they would be facing soon enough.

"Sure." Sean looked down at the severed hand sign and changed directions accordingly.

Quinn grabbed his arm, and they quickened their pace ahead of the others. Selah closely observed them together. It infuriated her every time that hell-witch touched her brother. She couldn't give away what Quinn was because God knew, Sean would have no idea what Selah was talking about, and she would end up looking like the crazy one. Selah hoped Quinn would reveal the ugly side of herself soon, otherwise Selah was going to have to bite the bullet and look crazy in order to save her brother.

They arrived at the "Freakish Ferris Wheel" as it was called. It stood over a hundred feet and looked like it was about to roll right off its axle. Tony grabbed Selah's hand instinctively and said, "We don't have to do this Say."

"No, I am no chicken." She gave a quick grin, then looked to Jaidyn. "You game?"

Jaidyn had a skeptical look on her face but nodded nonetheless.

Standing in line, they watched in disgust as Sean and Quinn kept kissing and joking around. It made Selah truly ill. Sean had absolutely no clue he was being toyed with by a demon.

Then it was Sean and Quinn's turn to climb into a seat. They waved down to Selah and them as they revolved only a quarter of the way up.

Next, it was their turn to climb on this rusted bucket of a ride. Selah said her second silent prayer of the night. This time a plea that they wouldn't die on this stupid ride before she had a chance to even face an enemy. She laughed at the possibility. How pathetic that would be after all her training.

Tony sat down first, Selah in the middle, feeling rather safe as Jaidyn squeezed in on the other side of her. It was a bit cramped, but it eased Selah's nerves.

Just as the Ferris wheel started, "Another One Bites the Dust" by Queen started playing through the speakers, and Selah rolled her eyes. If her nerves weren't already on high alert she would have laughed.

Tony chuckled and winked at her. Luckily, the music drowned out the creaking, so there was that. Jaidyn groaned, and when Selah saw why, she hugged her friend's arm. They had a clear view, yet again, of Quinn and Sean making out. In an attempt to take her attention away from it Selah asked, "What do you think Quinn is going to have us do while the boys are picking up this mysterious package?"

"Make us slaves and take over the world," Jaidyn grumbled. "Or turn us into toads."

Tony laughed heartily, which caught Sean and Quinn's attention.

When they turned back around, Jaidyn stuck her tongue out at the back of their heads. "Selah, when we finally get a chance to kick some demon butt, I know you really should get first dibs on beating Quinn, but please just let me get one shot in."

Selah chuckled and patted her arm. "Okay, it's a deal."

The "Freakish Ferris Wheel" finally screeched to a stop, and Sean and Quinn got out first, waiting, then the rest of them hopped off as soon as their seat stopped rocking.

"All right, y'all." Quinn quirked a smile and laced her arms with both Selah and Jaidyn.

Selah cringed inside.

"Time for us girls to go have fun. Hurry up, boys, and get Luc's package so we can meet up with him and get back to our night of fun," Quinn purred.

"Wait, we have to meet him somewhere? Can't he just wait till tomorrow?" Sean sounded disappointed that their night would be interrupted.

"Yeah, silly, I thought I told you." She tried to look innocent, but Selah saw right through it. Sean not so much.

"Fine." Then he looked at Tony. "Let's hurry this up then."

"Meet us back by the entrance in like thirty." Quinn smiled, then dragged them off in the opposite direction.

Selah looked back to Tony, who gave her a reassuring smile. She was confident he would watch after Sean and could protect them both from whatever evil they might face.

Quinn let go of them for a minute, apparently to text Luc and let him know they would be done soon.

She took them to a not-so-funhouse. Selah really wasn't game. But she and Jaidyn followed Quinn inside. Immediately, they were bombarded by screaming ghouls and crazy-eyed clowns, and chased half way into the funhouse.

Selah hated haunted houses with a passion; this one was definitely no exception. They turned a corner as she walked into a seething, tar-skinned, onyx-eyed demon. A Shadow-Walker. She nearly cussed, as she turned around and Quinn and Jaidyn weren't there. She reached behind her back for her blades but her arms froze at her side.

Nightmares began to plague her mind. She screamed, and the demon's razor-sharp claws met her flesh, ripping into her shoulder, breaking her mind free of the nightmare. She gripped both blades. They instantaneously lit up. The Shadow-Walker screeched in agony. Selah lashed out and impaled it in the chest with both blades. She whispered into the demon's ear, "Jesus."

The monster's lightless eyes bulged and in a blast of ash the Shadow-Walker disappeared.

She dropped to both knees, sheathed her blades at her back, and began to shake. She heard Jaidyn scream. She ran to her and began fussing over her. Quinn looked unconcerned as Jaidyn put Selah's arm over her shoulder, trying to drag her out of the funhouse and heal her at the same time. The wounds weren't healing, at least not at the rate Jaidyn normally could heal her.

Selah sighed faintly. She was losing so much blood.

They were out of earshot when Sean began confessing to Tony. "I really think that Quinn has some sort of hold on me or something. It's hard to explain, but when I am with her, it's like she coils herself around my brain and can't think straight. All I think about is her and making her happy, but I keep feeling this tug on me, like Selah is right next to me telling me to wake up. What if I can't do this thing Luc wants me to do?" Sean continued to wring his hands as he pressed on. He was interrupted by a text from Quinn, one she forwarded from Luc. It was a picture of Elizabeth. Sean nearly choked and stopped walking. Shaking, he handed his phone to Tony. From the looks of it, Elizabeth was unconscious, strapped to a chair.

Then another text with a photo pinged on his phone. It was a picture of Selah sprawled on the ground with Jaidyn over her looking frantic, and blood seeping into the ground beneath her. The actual text attached read: *Make it quick.*

Tony stared ahead at the haunted house they needed to enter and handed the phone to Sean.

Sean blanched and gripped the phone so tight he nearly cracked the screen. "What if I fail them, Tone?" He groaned a deep sigh, raking his hair with his free hand.

Before Tony could answer he continued. "I have been so freaking blind. The drugs and Quinn have flooded my mind, so much so that working for Luc just felt natural, but this..." He looked at the phone.

"I should have known better. My dad would be so disappointed with me right now." He began to walked faster toward the haunted house.

Tony felt the heavy truth of Sean's words. He was right; Dean would have been furious that he let this happen to Selah and Elizabeth, but even he would have acknowledged the pain that started this all. It was a travesty that Sean's dad was killed by a drug dealer, then for Sean to end up getting hooked on drugs, which he took to numb the pain from missing his dad. Grief is a heavy thing. Not dealing with it leads to a vicious cycle. Tony realized he could have gone down this road too when his parents died, but he'd luckily found motorcycles and made the decision to stay clean and sober.

"We just need to get that stupid shipment." Tony let out a long, deep sigh, releasing all his tension. He decided now was the time for Sean to learn the truth. Tony was about to shatter his reality. Tony remembered what Gabriel had said about breaking the truth to the others influenced by succubi, so he forged ahead, praying God would give him the appropriate words.

"Sean." They continued walking beside each other. "There are some things I am going to have to breakdown for you. Some things that sound absolutely crazy. Like a strange sci-fi show or something, but I promise you brother to brother here, what I am about to tell you is the absolute truth. And I have heard that the truth can set you free." He weakly smiled at his feeble joke, then marched on to tell Sean about the influence that Anne-Marie almost had on him and that Quinn had a similar form of control on Sean. Then he explained exactly what Quinn and Anne-Marie were.

"Wait, wait, wait." Sean gawked at him, shaking his head in disbelief. "I have been sleeping with a demon?"

Tony met Sean's eyes, frowning, and tilted his head in a sharp nod. "Sorry, buddy. We tried to tell ya."

"You didn't tell me she was a free-will-killing succubus!"

"You got me there." Tony shrugged. "Though would you have believed us before?"

Sean's shoulders slumped. "Probably not."

Tony championed on breaking the rest of the news, that Tony, Selah, Jaidyn, and Daniel were Chosen by God with some special purpose. He explained that the night of Daniel's death triggered their intense training by the Angels, how they had to learn about the different demons that linger in this world and hangout around AfterBurn. *Oh yes, let's not forget.* "Also, um, we work for the Lord of the Underworld himself. Luc Vega, is actually better known as Lucifer."

Sean had had enough. Tony could see the information overload was about to completely make Sean lose his mental capacity. *Maybe I should stop.*

"You can't be serious...First, I become addicted to a demon drug, then I falsely fall in love with one, and now I am apparently working for Lucifer himself?"

"Yep, that pretty much sums it up." Tony raised his brows in surprise at how well Sean was taking this.

"Hold up..." Tony watched Sean, concerned as he walked off the path a bit. Tony waited as Sean stumbled into the bushes, falling to his knees and heaving up the pretzel he just paid for.

"Sean, you okay?"

Sean came back, running his tongue over his teeth, and spit, then began walking.

"Oh sure, never better."

Tony was glad to see Sean's sarcasm hadn't died.

CHAPTER 41

SEAN

At the entrance of the "House of Horrors," the major haunted house attraction, the doors were well guarded by two humanoid looking gargoyles. They looked to be in costume, but with the news he just received, Sean couldn't be certain. He stood up straighter, trying to have a commanding look. "I am here on behalf of Luc Vega to pick up a package." The gargoyles nodded to each other than opened the door. Sean noted there was no one else at this attraction—even when Tony went to walk in with him the guarding gargoyles barred him from entering.

Tony's eyes widened. Sean followed his glance as it landed on another door farther inside lit by red flashing lights, and blocked by a tall broad-shouldered demon. Sean could swear it was recognition on Tony's face. Sean heard him say, "Trust no one in there. Be careful. I will be waiting and make it quick or I am coming in after you."

Sean's back went rigid again, and he turned to face his mission.

Jaidyn screamed at Quinn, "Get out of my way!"

Quinn stood nonchalantly, looking at her nails. "Sorry, precious. I can't do that. Luc's orders."

Jaidyn stood face-to-face with the hell-witch. "Listen, I know what you are, and I am not afraid of you. If we don't get her help, you will soon learn to be afraid of me!" Jaidyn stood back, ripping her heart-jeweled pendant from her neck. She pressed the gem between the wings, and the mace unfolded quickly.

Quinn's eyes showed no mercy. "Oh, you want to play, little girl?" Quinn's nails elongated as she placed her feet into a fighting stance.

"We don't have time to squabble. Selah needs attention now!"

At the last syllable, Quinn pounced toward Jaidyn. When both Jaidyn's hands wrapped around the hilt of the mace, the razor wings sprung out. Jaidyn batted her down. The impact made a sickening crunch into Quinn's ribs. Quinn looked down at her abdomen and hissed.

"What did you do?" Quinn's blood ran black. Her skin began to show its true sickly color, her eyes black with rage.

"Told you. Now. I am getting Selah help!" Jaidyn picked up Selah, heavier with near unconsciousness.

"Luc will have your head for this," Quinn yelled at her back.

Jaidyn ignored her as she half carried, half dragged Selah to the gated exit of Inferno.

Quinn went to follow, but stepped back into Inferno's entrance when she saw the Angels step out from the shadows outside the gate to meet Jaidyn. They stood near Selah's car. Jaidyn looked over her shoulder, glaring back at Quinn and roared, "Go to hell!"

Sean walked up to the statuesque demon. "Um...hi." Sean gulped then sputtered out the rest. "I'm supposed to pick something up for Luc Vega."

"We have been waiting for you, Son of Adam." Sean looked confused. His dad's name was Dean. Then he shook his head, remembering how upside down everything was. The biblical reference hit him like a fist to the face. How far he had fallen, quite like Adam.

The demon continued. "We miss the Luc here in the Inferno. I am Abaddon," he huffed. "I will be escorting you to make sure nothing goes wrong." When he smirked at Sean, his teeth were as sharp as a shark's. Surprisingly, they did not cut his lips or make him bleed when he grinned like that. Sean leaned away a bit.

"Okay," was all Sean could get out before Abaddon started again.

"Come on in." He opened the door for Sean. As soon as he walked in, the air was stifling. Warm, rank, and thick. Sean coughed.

"You'll get used to it soon enough." He walked ahead of Sean. Sean tried to walk casually, but his footsteps felt as if they were trudging through mud. He watched Abaddon walk with no issue and tried desperately to quicken his steps.

They reached a hall of mirrors. Sean noticed Abaddon's reflection. He was already tall with red-pocked skin, but in his reflection, Sean saw horns spouting out each side of his head, curling over his ears like ram horns. His body was overly brutish, and though fully dressed, the mirror showed that he was naked except for a ragged black cloth that hung over his hips. The rest of him was covered in smears of dirt and blood.

Sean heard the overhead music and tried not to hysterically laugh. "Highway to Hell" blared through the hall of mirrors. His breath hitched sharply when he caught his own reflection. Sean's body was covered in deep-grey skin, pockmarked like Abaddon's, but his eyes were his own, and his clothes were intact. His face was covered in thorns of all sizes and the horns on his forehead were barely larger than the thorns themselves. He closed his eyes and shook his head; it didn't make a difference. When he opened his eyes again the same reflection stared back at him.

Abaddon made his way to another door way, when Tom Petty's "I Won't Back Down" began playing. It gave Sean the resolve he needed. He would do this, for his mom and sister, whether it killed him or broke his unsteady mind.

They walked through the last door where the air was sickly—full of sulfur and death. All around them were piles and piles of bones. At the end of the room was a desk. A demon much shorter than Abaddon stood.

"We have been waiting for you." The other demon said callously.

Abaddon spoke, "Well, here he is. Let's get this over with." He glared at this other demon with contempt.

"Introductions first." He paused to look Sean over. "Luc sure knows how to pick the broken ones doesn't he?" He glanced back at Abaddon with mirth in his smile. Abaddon rolled his eyes, then crossed his arms over his chest. "Okay, okay."

Sean was astonished at how precisely the music in this "House of Horrors" matched the situation. As he left the other room, he could hear "Crazy Train" playing. He wondered if he had already hitched a ride on that train himself.

"I am Mammon. Most know me as Envy, but you can call me Ramon, all the mortals do." He grinned a toothy smile. Only, his teeth were white and bright, and very human, nothing like Abaddon's. He put his hand out for Sean to shake. Sean took his hand tentatively. "So, you're here for the package, huh?" He looked over Sean unconvinced. "I hope you make it through the last leg of this trek. Most don't. But...I am sure good ol' Luci didn't tell you that." He gave a wink. "Anyway." He gestured to Abaddon to go open the door in the back of the catacomb-like office.

Sean watched Abaddon. He uncrossed his arms, stomped over to the door, and flung it open. Flames and methane came gusting into the doorway. "Well, Son of Adam, time for you to walk through hellfire. At the end of the walkway will be two cases—take only the two cases. It doesn't surprise me that Luci wanted to stay on Earth, otherwise, I would have gladly switched places." He spun around with his arms stretched out. "But I get to be in charge down here for a while." He shooed Sean out the door. "Hurry, go! Can't waste precious time."

Sean walked to the door where Abaddon was waiting, then peered back at Ramon. His eyes lit up with the green flames of pure want. Sean could see the envy buried deep within him and quickly turned back toward the open doorway of flames.

Abaddon stepped in first.

Sean followed.

As soon as Sean's foot hit the threshold his skin burned like battery acid had been poured over it. He groaned against the pain. He inspected his arm. It was changing to the grey-pocked skin he'd seen in the mirror earlier. As he stepped farther in, his mind became muddled with the sheer pain and the cries of the dead.

Abaddon said something, but Sean couldn't understand him. When he reached up both hands to his head as if to gather his wits, Sean felt the horns then the spikes all over his flesh, which gave an electric shock through his skull when he hit them. He cried out, "Jesus!" Suddenly, his knees hit the ground—so did Abaddon's.

Abaddon thundered in disapproval. Sean didn't know why. It took a moment of silence before Abaddon could get himself off the steaming stone floor beneath him. He lumbered over to Sean, bellowing, "That name is forbidden down here! We only have one master, and he is not one of them. If Ramon heard you, you would be dead!"

Sean grimaced as he tried to get up, his bare hands burning against the stone. He stood.

"Got it! Would have helped to know that before I stepped in here," Sean argued.

"Hey, kid, you're the first one to actually cross the doorway."

Sean froze. What did that say about him? Was he a demon? Was that why he was changing into this thing? All he knew was he needed to get the hell out of Hell. He trudged on, ready to be done and get those wretched cases.

When he found an alcove that wasn't burning, he spotted the black cases. They gleamed in the flames. They looked like large travel cases covered in some kind of lightweight metal. Sean tried to lift one, and to his surprise, he lifted it without the help of his second arm. Quinn said he would need Tony's help.

He knew he had gotten stronger since taking Doxy, but he still expected to some kind of struggle, especially with how large the cases were.

A humongous demon with a cape of flames and a skull of steaming iron walked toward Abaddon. His voice sounded like gravel being tumbled, but Abaddon understood him. "We are here to get Lucifer's weapons," he answered then saluted to the huge fire and rock monster.

Sean got the other case and started stepping carefully back toward the door they came through.

Abaddon said nonchalantly, "General Tarok needed my verification. He and the other Generals of Hell worked tirelessly on those weapons to just give them up to some no-name beast, or human, for that matter."

Sean cocked his head to the side. "Weapons? I thought I was grabbing some demon drug or alcohol."

Abaddon's brows rose. "Hmm, I thought Luc told ya. Oh well, ya know now."

Sean shook his head. He had to do this. For Selah and Mom, but he had no idea what Luc was up to with these Hell-made weapons. Out of all the things he knew about the Bible, he sure hoped he wasn't helping bring on some apocalypse or something. Sean swallowed hard. The air was getting really thin, and the doorway seemed like it was moving further away from him. Sean's grip was starting to slip. Abaddon eyed him suspiciously. Sean wouldn't fail. He would not die here.

Finally, he started making headway when his lungs felt like they were about to collapse. He felt like he was drowning in fire. Five feet from the door his skin started turning back to normal, and when he got back through the door to the catacombs-style office, he dropped the cases so he could feel his face, silently thanking God. He'd made it, and he wasn't forever trapped as a prisoner in Hell.

He sighed in relief.

Ramon clapped excitedly as he greeted Sean back. "You made it!" He looked at Abaddon, "Can you believe it?"

"Not really, and I was there the whole time." Abaddon almost looked impressed. "Come on, let's get you on your way."

Abaddon walked him back out the way he came in. Still, no one was in line for this attraction. Sean saw Tony waiting by the entrance. Behind his head he saw the "Attraction Permanently Closed for Repair" sign. *Huh, I must have missed that.*

Tony looked over Sean's head toward Abaddon with murder in his eyes. Sean looked back to Abaddon who had a look of recognition on his own face. Sean hurried to get to Tony, and get far away from this place. "What was that about?"

Tony grumbled, "That lowlife demon killed my parents."

Sean caught Tony's eye. "I'm sorry Tone, we have to go."

Tony understood, or at least didn't push the issue, so Sean started walking through the two gargoyles and out the door. He handed one of the cases to Tony, who strained a bit to keep a grip on it.

"Damn, Sean, what's in this thing?"

"I'm told it's weapons, but I didn't look. Let's just go get Mom and help Selah." Tony heaved the case while Sean continued to carry his effortlessly.

"Give it to me," Sean said.

Tony did gratefully.

"How can you carry both of those?"

"Honestly, dude, I think it's the drugs."

"At least they are helpful for once," Tony joked.

Sean was grateful that Tony was with him in all this craziness. Otherwise, Sean was sure he would have lost his mind about an hour ago.

Tony perked up. "Oh, I mean to tell ya, Selah is with Jaidyn, and they are safe with the Angels. I didn't ask about Quinn, sorry."

"No worries. I couldn't care less at the moment."

Just before they reached the exit, Sean spotted her blonde hair. *Speak of the devil.* She was waiting by the main entrance.

She spoke up as they moved in closer. "I'm supposed to escort you to Luc."

Sean deadpanned, unsure how to respond. Then she turned and sashayed out the exit, not waiting for them to follow.

Tony's brow lifted in question, "You okay Sean? Like can you feel her in your head right now?"

"Nope." Sean shrugged effortlessly.

"Good," Tony said as they followed her. Sean laid the cases in the trunk. He wasn't ready to deal with Quinn, but he was ready to face Luc and trade these ghastly weapons for his mom.

•   C H A P T E R   4 2   •

JUDAS

Luc commanded the Shadow-Walker to get on its knees and beg for forgiveness, faulted for the failure of his subordinate. Luc wasted no time—a quick, sickening slice to the neck and a thud as the Shadow-Walker hit the floor. Black, tarry blood pooled on the ground. The leader of the Shadow-Walkers lay dead. It's lifeless form immediately disintegrating, the ashes floating away and disappearing in thin air.

"Dammit, Judas!" He wiped his sharp stiletto blade as if he was casually cleaning a pair of glasses.

Judas's eyes went wide, pure black, filled with frustration and confusion.

Luc's accusing stare was full of fire as he slicked back his salt-and-pepper grey hair making sure no hair was out of place. He took off his white cloth gloves carefully as the finger tips were covered in bloody tar. Luc disposed of them in the waste basket and calmly stroked his highly maintained beard to make sure no blood had splattered on his face.

With a look of pure disgust, his attention was back on Judas. "I gave your idiot Shadow-Walkers one job. One job! And they can't even do that right! Why in hell am I still dealing with you? Seems no one can do a job right anymore." He moved to lean against his mahogany desk in the only office of his warehouse. He crossed his muscular arms across his chest. Luc's delicate neck snapping hands rested on his upper arms. He seemed to be contemplating something Judas was not allowed in on. "You will clean this mess up, then next time be sure to find someone capable of handling a mark. Obviously not a Shadow-Walker; they are only good to scare the hell into people. They feed off fear not death. Next time maybe think about trying any one of the many demon assassins if the job is that damn hard!"

Judas shifted his weight under Luc's heavy stare. "We know Selah is badly wounded. We could send someone to kill her now."

"No! My shipment is almost here. She is obviously trained now and armed!" His voice raised an octave. "Quinn also saw her leave with the Angels, so your chances of success have now dwindled considerably." Luc's glare bored into Judas.

Judas flinched like Luc had slapped him in the face. He carefully looked Luc in the eye. "Yes, you are right, sir. What would you like me to do when I am done with this?" He pointed toward what was left of the ashes and blood.

"Elizabeth is unconscious downstairs. I think I will use this to my advantage. Sean should be here soon. With Quinn's influence on him we may be able to manipulate it in our favor." Luc eyed Judas like a scared puppy about to hide under a couch. Judas would prove he wasn't useless to Luc, otherwise, he would soon look like the mess he was cleaning.

He shuddered.

Judas needed to get his crap together if he wanted to rule under Luc, but at this rate, he would be lucky if Lucifer kept him in this realm and didn't send him back to Hell.

"If this doesn't work, I will do it my damn self. I am tired of loose ends. The Chosen should have been destroyed long ago when they were of no threat to my plans. Now, now, I know for sure the angels are in this hole-in-the-wall-town, and they are now working together." He took a breath then growled, "I want results, Asmodeus! Results!"

Luc retired to his smoking room next to the office. Before he shut the door, he growled, "Clean this up quick. We have little time before the weapons arrive."

Judas knew that Luc hated getting his hands dirty. This was why he had a handful of lower demons around, to do his dirty work. He was far too civilized for this. He was a manipulator. He killed virtues and dreams, but he loved breaking the human psyche far more than drawing blood, which could be done by anyone. Judas hoped this plan of Luc's would work. If it didn't Judas and the others would suffer his wrath.

He lit a cigar and poured himself a hefty glass of single-malt scotch from a bygone era. Luc puffed on his Cuban as he tried to calm his anger. Now was not the time for this mayhem; he needed these weapons from Hell and that was his top priority. Especially now that this small band of would-be-heroes were working with the Angels. With these unearthly weapons, he would have an advantage if any Angel of God's Army came for him. Sean had been Luc's last attempt to get these weapons, and luckily the Doxy had protected him long enough to get them. Sean had been the last guinea pig in a long line of failed attempts. Luc was satisfied that one of his plans had not failed, he took another swig of scotch.

Luc was ready to be out of this form. Though he liked his rugged, distinguished good-looks, he hated how cumbersome it felt to walk and talk in flesh. He wanted to be seen by the world in his true form, in all his magnificent glory. He wanted this human race, the beloved of God to see his mighty power and worship him as if he was their God. Oh, what a sweet joy that would be, to turn the heads of the ones who once dearly loved their Maker. He would be humanity's undoing, and he couldn't wait to relish in it.

His only obstacle now was finding the Angels. He knew of a few Cherubim that worked the area because they dispatched a few of his men back to Hell. He knew the higher Angels were here, and that they were currently with Selah. He wondered if they would intervene on Sean's behalf or stay with one of the Chosen. He needed to keep them from fouling up his plans. Luc set his mind on the next phase, to pluck out the Angels and the Chosen from Earth one by one.

Asmodeus called from the other room, announcing he was done cleaning up Luc's mess. Luc smiled. What a good lapdog.

"They are here." Judas gestured to the downstairs holding bay. Elizabeth was still out. She originally came to once she got there, but with some finesse, she was currently a very agreeable prisoner. Luc buttoned then straightened his suit jacket and began sauntering down the stairs, watching as Quinn walked in. "Where is Sean?"

"Right here," Sean called up as he brought in the cases on his own. To Luc's surprise, Tony, his bartender, walked in behind Sean. Luc glared at Quinn for her omission.

"We have a guest I see. How unfortunate. Quinathra, why didn't you tell me we had a guest coming?"

"Sorry, Lord." She ducked her head.

"As you should be," he huffed. "Well, hello again, Anthony. That is your given name, correct?"

Tony gave a curt nod.

"Great. Well, you can see I don't have time for pleasantries. Sean, bring me the cases." He waved Sean over.

Sean froze.

"Come on, boy, I don't have all day. Do you want your mother back or not?" His expression boiled with rage.

Sean slowly began to walk toward him.

When Lucifer made a move toward Sean, his accomplice lit up like the dawn with flames licking his arms, but incredibly it didn't burn him.

Judas jumped back when he realized it was Holy Fire.

Lucifer growled, "I had my suspicions." He stepped away from Sean. "You're one of them."

Sean looked at his friend with awe.

"Then follow me to the office will you! Let's not waste any more time." Luc was running rather impatient, even more than he normally did.

Judas craved seeing these weapons that made Lucifer so damn jumpy. They had to be something incredible.

·   CHAPTER 43   ·

MICHAEL

Michael and Raphael had been stationed outside Selah's house. They, unfortunately had to watch as
Elizabeth was kidnapped so they could follow Luc's
goons to his apparent safe house or warehouse. Gabriel and Uriel had gone on to follow Selah and the
others in hopes of protecting them from any harm
while at Inferno. For all it was worth, Michael tried
to contemplate why exactly Luc needed Sean to go
into Inferno; he had so many servants who would
gladly do his bidding for him.

As Michael and Raphael watched Luc's men drive
off with Elizabeth, they did not hesitate to follow.
Michael radioed to Uriel. "We are leaving the Moore

home. They have Elizabeth. We are following them now. Good luck, Brother."

✦ ✦ ✦

Uriel and Gabriel helped Selah slump into the car's backseat.

Uriel looked at Gabriel.

Gabriel nodded and got in the driver seat of Selah's car.

Uriel watched Tony and Sean leave with Quinn in a different car. Before he started his motorcycle, he radioed to Michael. "We have our eye on them. God speed."

✦ ✦ ✦

They were all on edge, especially equipped with the cryptic vision God had shown them about tonight's mission and its possible casualties. Michael was most determined of all to not see anything bad happen to Selah. Not today, or any day soon, but of course the decision was not his. He trusted Uriel and

Gabriel would be just as diligent. Neither of them wanted to lose another charge. He prayed for God to bring peace to his anxious heart. God alone knew the plan that the Chosen had to accomplish for Heaven. Michael would not question it.

Michael raced through side streets and tried to remain undetected by Luc's driver and his accomplices. Michael was thankful for his time on the police force, for his God-given battle strategies, because currently they were helping him navigate these back roads.

Michael looked over at Raphael, who in serene silence was keeping a sharp eye out for any unexpected turns taken by the van up ahead. Raphael looked lethal in her head-to-toe tactical gear. Strapped on the outside of both of her legs were her twin daggers, Athriel and Ithriel, her beloved Angel blades forged by the fires of the Seraphim and blessed by God himself. Michael's sword was the one weapon handed down by God, given specifically to Michael to cast down Lucifer to the pits of Hell. While in the human realm the sword seemed rather short and unimportant, when Michael whispered it's given name, Zedekiah, the Blade of Justice, then the lackluster blade flared to life in a living, raging, holy, impurity-stripping fire. Michael smiled at the thought of using the sword once again. He looked into the rearview mirror at his sheath belt hanging in the back. A belt and blade he had worn for millennia.

They turned a corner, and the van pulled quickly onto a rocky driveway leading to a row of nondescript warehouses. Only one of the buildings had a light on, like a beacon in the night. Michael silenced the engine as he and Raph both watched and waited. Luc's men roughly grabbed the no longer unconscious Elizabeth with duct tape over her mouth. The lackeys had a vise grip on her and began heading towards the lit-up warehouse.

"Lucifer is either cocky, or he really doesn't know how closely involved we are with the Chosen." Raphael shook her head.

"Knowing him it could be an invitation." Michael caught her eye and arched a brow.

"True." Her mouth quirked in a sideways smile.

They waited till they were inside, except for the driver, who seemed to be stationed at the ready in case of a quick escape. He would be their first target.

They climbed out of Raph's car and shut the doors far more quietly than probably necessary and stayed in the shadows as they made their way to the back of the van. Their abilities gave them stealth, but they made sure to pay extra attention to keep the rocky driveway from giving them away.

With a flash of movement, Michael knocked out the driver in one swift punch, being careful to not oversaturate his powers and knock the poor guy's head in. The driver slumped to the side, blood dripping from his nose, but still breathing. Raph caught Michael's eye from the back of the van and pointed toward the roof. From there they would be able to get a good view of what was happening inside.

Raphael approached first and gave the all clear. Michael followed up the flimsy ladder, only bolts and screws keeping it connected to the side of the warehouse. Michael was not nearly as lean as Raphael and could swear he heard the metal groan a bit under his muscled girth, making him climb more quickly.

Once on the roof, they scanned looking for an entryway, and saw a roof access door. Gingerly they creeped to the canopy windows over the work area of the warehouse. They peered down through the grungy windows. They could see an office, tucked in the back corner. No one was in sight.

Michael looked at Raph and whispered the plan of entry. "From the roof door there is a loft. It looks empty. We will enter there. Let's see how close we can get to that office. I would wager a guess that is where Luc is."

Raphael saluted. They headed back toward the roof access. Before opening the rusted old door, Raph oiled the joints. Smiling, Michael thought she was rather clever always traveling with anointing oil. "Good thinking."

Michael carefully opened the door. By the grace of God, it made no noise. He made his way in. Raphael followed and shut the door without a sound. Michael's flesh was tingling with anticipation as they covertly continued through the warehouse. *Where are all of Lucifer's guards?*

Then he saw them on the lower level—guards around a table eating dinner but no sign of Luc or the two who came in with Elizabeth. They held back and watched from the shadows precisely at the moment Luc came out of the office. "You imbeciles, get back to work! What do you think I pay you for?" It wasn't a question, they all knew that.

Each guard pushed away from the table. One held back and grabbed a slice of ham off the six-foot sub they had been eating. Five guards in total, only two were coming up the loft stairs headed toward the roof entrance.

The guards didn't know what hit them; a black blurry mass with blond hair incapacitated them with two sleeping darts imbedded into each of their necks. These men were mortal hoodlums, likely working for money or drugs. Raphael wasn't one to harm a human, and with precision, neither of the darts nicked any major bleeders.

Michael's head turned back toward the room when he heard Sean's voice. "Right here."

● CHAPTER 44 ●

SELAH

Her anguish came out in a sigh. The pain was searing her from the inside out. She looked into Jaidyn's eyes pleading, "We need to go after Sean." It was not a request. She hoped Jaidyn understood that. Selah wasn't about to let Sean and Tony face Lucifer on their own, especially since Sean had no weapons, no training, and last she saw him, he was hopped up on Doxy.

Uriel had come to Selah's other side, helping Jaidyn get her in the car. Gabriel helped too. Uriel caught her eye. "Selah, you're badly injured. We need to get you to the safe house and get you patched up. For some reason Jaidyn's powers aren't working against the Shadow-Walker's wound."

Uriel's words didn't quell Selah's determination. "I need to help my brother. How quick can you patch me up?" She groaned.

"If Gabriel can get us to the safe house fast enough, it will only take me a few minutes to grab what we need, then we can head in Sean's direction as I patch you up." Jaidyn continued to try to heal Selah's injury, but all she could do at this moment was staunch her bleeding.

Once Gabriel got behind the steering wheel and started the car, he punched the gas and made a bee-line for the church.

Each bump and turn Selah could feel ripping through her arm and shoulder. She glanced at her wounded arm, begging it to heal. She saw her veins turning black, snaking down to her hand. "Hey, Gabe, I thought Shadow-Walkers would only feed on fears." She tried to breathe through the pain.

"This one must have been sent to harm you. It may be some sort of poison. When we meet up with Raphael, she should be able to tell us. Just hold on kid." He continued to race through the streets.

They finally made it to the parking lot of the old church. Jaidyn jumped out with the keys Gabriel had given her. She came back with an armful of bandages and ointments of various kinds. She tossed the keys back to Gabriel. Uriel waited on his motorcycle at the edge of the sidewalk, ready to lead them when they got back on the road.

Gabriel followed Uriel, who's voice came on over the radio. "Raphael gave me the address before they went to investigate the warehouse. It shouldn't take us long. It is on this side of town but on the outskirts of the city."

Gabriel responded, "Okay, just show us the way."

Jaidyn used some gauze with hydrogen peroxide, but despite it not being rubbing alcohol it still burned like hell. Selah bit her lip to keep from screaming, and a low groan escaped instead. "I'm sorry, Say. I'm trying not to hurt you."

"I know, I know. This sucker just burns like nobody's business."

Jaidyn caught Gabriel's eye in the rearview mirror; both of them looked worried. Selah was not about to read too much into it. She just needed to get to her brother. She would be fine. Jaidyn continued her ministrations as she carefully wound the gauze around her arm and shoulder.

"Can you still use your arm?" she inquired.

Selah lifted it slowly, opening and closing her fist and turning it from side to side. With each movement she felt the burning, grinding pain, but she could at least use it if she needed. She painfully mumbled, "Yeah, I think it will be okay."

They had turned onto another street when Uriel came in again, "Okay, Gabe, park quietly, lights out. You see Raph's car?"

Gabriel looked about. "Yep, I see it now." Then he turned off his headlights and pulled in Selah's car quietly behind Raphael's. Uriel turned off his motorcycle and quickly pushed it over between the two vehicles. Uriel walked to the back-passenger door and opened it for Selah. "You okay, lass?"

Selah took her time getting out of the back and whispered, "Yeah, I am fine."

"Good." Without delay, he rattled on. "Here is the plan. You and Jaidyn act like you just happened to find the place. If you stumble in looking for your brother on your own, we have more of a chance of an ambush."

"Okay," she and Jaidyn said together.

"God is with you. You have your weapons?" Jaidyn took her pendant out of her pocket and Selah patted her back.

"Yep," in unison once again. They smiled at each other, then Selah said, "We are ready for this, well, as ready as we will ever be."

"All right." Gabriel looked at Uriel. "We will meet up with Michael and Raphael on the roof."

"Stay strong, remember your training."

Selah's arm pulsed as she nodded, and she and Jaidyn progressed toward Luc's warehouse.

Uriel watched the warehouse as the girls approached. A light inside caught his eyes. He closed his eyes for a moment to change his ability to see the spiritual realm. When he opened them again, he saw past the walls of the warehouse. Lucifer in his demon form was within feet of Sean and Tony. Tony's arms were flaming with Holy Fire, and Asmodeus was stepping away from the small crowd, likely as far away from the fire as he could get. Suddenly, their attention changed to the warehouse door. Uriel smiled with pride for Tony but knew their diverted attention was his and Gabriel's cue to continue on and meet up with the Michael and Raphael.

"Hey Mikey, we are here. Where are you?" He gave a clear whisper into his radio.

Michael whispered his answer, "Loft inside the lit-up warehouse."

Uriel and Gabriel both headed toward the ladder that led to the roof.

Michael's voice broke into the silence. "Head up to the roof access door. We already neutralized the threat up there." Uriel held back long enough to watch Tony and Sean gather the cases and walk them into Luc's office.

They made it up to the roof, then followed the trail of incapacitated bodies to find Michael and Raph waiting in the shadows. They were peering through the loft window down to the office door downstairs.

Michael turned, sensing Uriel's presence. "Tony and Sean just walked into the office."

Uriel nodded his acknowledgement.

They looked down when they heard Jaidyn and Selah run into the warehouse screaming, "Sean! Tony! Where are you?" The few guards left downstairs couldn't make out what was going on.

"I demand you let me see them," Jaidyn commanded as Selah continued to call out their names.

"Sean! Tony!"

One of the guards went to grab Jaidyn. She grabbed his wrist and wrestled his arm behind his back. The other guard looked shocked but decided to get Selah before she could do the same. His plan was thwarted the instant Uriel jumped down from the stairs and punched him in the jaw. When and if he woke up, he wouldn't be talking any time soon.

Michael, Raph, and Gabriel followed Uriel down, but not nearly as dramatically. Luc's guards came out from inside the office to check the commotion as planned.

Michael, in a quick motion, pummeled one on top of the head, he crumpled like a castle made of playing cards.

The other guard took a swing at Raphael. She dodged the blow in a swift motion, and in quick succession kicked his leg out from under him, wrapped her arm around his neck and inserted a tranquilizer dart.

Jaidyn walked into the office. Selah dragged herself in behind her, her shoulder bandages now soaking with blood. Jaidyn still had Luc's last standing guard in her firm grip.

Uriel had to give it to her for a petite young lady Jaidyn sure was strong. Michael, Raphael, Gabriel and at last Uriel stepped into the office. Selah's eyes goggled in pure panic when she saw Elizabeth was bleeding from her scalp, like she had been hit in the head. She was slouched in the chair. Uriel had forgotten to tell Selah that Elizabeth had been kidnapped. Inwardly, he groaned.

Sean caught sight of Jaidyn holding the guard hostage and paled.

Tony looked relieved when his eyes caught Selah's.

Luc grinned wickedly when he saw his estranged siblings. "Hello, Brother." His eyes pierced into Michael.

• CHAPTER 45 •

MICHAEL

Luc continued to smile, gritting his teeth when he said, "Well, now that we are all here." Quinn got up from the chair behind his desk and sauntered over to Lucifer's side. He continued. "I'm so glad you all could make it for the unveiling of my newly prized toys." His maniacal laugh grated Michael's nerves.

Quinn walked back to the large mahogany desk where the cases had been laid open. She pulled out a black matte steel blade, one side curved wickedly sharp, the other serrated. Down the hilt, cracks feathered and were filled with what looked like molten lava.

Uriel and the others paled.

Michael piqued. They needed to get them all out of here and quick.

"Oh, see, I had an inkling the Chosen would bring their masters here with them. In fact, I was quite hoping for this very occasion." Lucifer, in a flurry of dark mist let loose his magnificent black angel wings, touched here and there with grey that matched his perfectly quaffed hair. "It has been too long since we have been reunited, don't you think, Michael?"

A chill hit the room as Lucifer looked into Michael's eyes and tilted his head. "Didn't think I would figure it out eventually? I am disappointed at how loose you have been with Selah's safety. I could have done this any time within the last few months. Sure, it took me awhile to piece it together. Selah was easy to pick out, being born the same day I came to this vapid realm. I knew you lot weren't far behind. I watched. I waited. Even had my men keep tabs on Selah and her family. And yet none of you have been thoroughly involved, that was until I sensed your presence at my club the night that young man, what was his name? Dave? Derek? Donald?"

Selah interrupted, wrath burning in her eyes. "Daniel!"

"Yes, Daniel. The night he was attacked. Stupid boy, had he just told us who the Chosen were in little ol' Gailton, he could have lived."

Selah's fists tightened by her side, her jaw twitched, and Michael could see the fury in her eyes.

Luc continued on, uncaring or unimpressed. "I knew my kin wouldn't be far, and now here we are." He threw out his arms indicating the entire group.

Michael forewarned, "Leave Selah and Elizabeth and the others out of this fight Lucifer, or I will take great pleasure in throwing you back into your pit."

"Touchy, touchy." He casually walked over to Michael with one of the wretched black blades in his hand. "What I haven't mentioned yet is these glorious toys." He displayed them in both hands for Michael to really take in. "They can bring pain, darkness, and devastation to the Angels before returning them back to the gates of Heaven."

For the first time ever, Michael saw fear etched on Uriel's face. Selah surveyed Michael, then the other Archangels to assess the truth of Luc's statement. Uriel pulled out Adara, the Guardian Sword of

Eden. It blazed to life in his grip. Lucifer's eyes caught on the sheer bright holiness of it. "I wouldn't get any closer if I were you, Brother."

Quinn walked over to Selah, who was barely standing up on her own two feet. Quinn grabbed her injured arm before Selah had a chance to pull away and held her with a bruising grip. Selah tried to fight her hold, but Quinn twisted and pulled at her violently.

Michael could see the pain written on her face. She walked Selah closer to the hell-made blades still out on display and picked up a stiletto black matte blade with a ribbon of that same lava-like substance, like Lucifer's blade, snaking through it. Selah huffed in frustration, looking over at Lucifer who winked at her. The Angels followed his eyes.

Quinn looked at Sean and ordered, "Kill her, Sean!"

"No!" Tony yelled, putting an arm out in front of Sean to stop him.

Sean glanced at Selah who was in so much pain her eyes barely stayed open. Then he caught Jaidyn's eye, her gaze begging him not to do it.

"No," Sean retorted.

In his hesitation, as the word formed on his lips, Quinn had already stabbed Selah in the ribs. Selah fell like lead weight to the ground. Screams erupted all around. Sean dropped next to his sister, crying and screaming at Lucifer, "You promised they wouldn't get hurt!"

"As I recall, it wasn't me who promised you anything..." Lucifer purred, giving Quinn a look of admiration.

In a flash of pure bright light, each of the Angels tore through their human forms. They stood like giants of pure radiant light in their full battle gear of the ancient Angel warriors, and were surrounded by strong, massive, glowing wings of white tipped with gold.

"Justice will come to you Lucifer," Michael thundered. In a blink of blinding light, they fled with all of the Chosen, Sean, and Elizabeth.

SELAH

Selah felt the blade pierce her skin, the sheer agony of it matching the burning pain in her shoulder. She was set ablaze in pain and anguish. She tried unsuccessfully to open her eyes, scream, or cry, only to make sure Sean and Mom weren't hurt. It didn't matter how hard she tried she couldn't open her eyes.

Immense peace poured over her making her body shudder. It was as if she had taken a deep, relieving breath. She was surrounded in warm radiant light. She gently tried to run her fingers through the light and noticed her fingers looked different—

unblemished and were glowing far brighter than she ever had before.

She looked down at her clothes. No longer was she wearing her battle gear and leather jacket. Instead, she was covered in the softest gown of pure woven light. The dress shimmered and sparkled as she moved.

Selah scanned her surroundings again, trying to get her bearings. She couldn't figure out where she was or how she got here. Her bare feet felt as if they were on solid ground, which was no different than the light that surrounded her.

A person emerged in the distance, his face a lot like Sean's, only it had been worn by time.

"Dad?" She hesitated.

"Yes, my girl." He continued to walk closer, then parted his lips in a deep smile when she ran to him. He held out his arms, embracing her tightly. Although his embrace didn't feel tight, instead it felt like sunsets, playing catch with him for little league, and his butterfly kisses at night.

"Oh, Star-Brite," he sighed.

She loved hearing that nickname. It was the name only he'd given her. He used to tell her she shined like the stars when she glowed.

"I have watched you become a beautiful young woman, but I have to tell you, you're not supposed to be here."

"Where are we? I mean, I am dreaming, right?"

He smiled, then held her hand with no answer. He walked her down a path of sparkling diamonds that headed toward more brilliant light. She turned when she heard her full name. "Selah Jane Moore, daughter of Elizabeth and Dean Moore, a Chosen one of God." It was a melodic voice that caressed her ears, one she remembered in her childhood dreams. The voice that called out to her in her darkest moments and simplest joys. It was Him, standing before her, Jesus Christ, himself.

"Selah, it is not your time to be here. Although I desire the day when we are reunited, God needs you to finish your race. Your destiny has not yet been fulfilled and the journey set before you must be completed. Be sure to listen to the Archangels, and continue to grow in strength. The influences of Lucifer in your family and city must be dealt with. Lucifer must be conquered and sent back to Hell."

A park bench materialized before them. Jesus sat down, inviting Selah to join him. "Lucifer wants nothing more than to encamp in the homes and cities of humanity. His first strategy usually starts in the home. Just like your dad's death, it was a way for Lucifer's influence to come into the heart of Sean. It weakened your mother's hope and faith, though Lucifer didn't count on it to strengthen your resolve. Truth is, he has tried to break you since the day you were born, but over and over again you have held true to God. Now, we have a gift for you."

Jesus, in his aura of peace and compassion, reached both of his scar-marred hands to her face, and held her tenderly. The storms that had ravaged her soul, the anger and frustration at her brother, the sadness she held deep inside from her dad's death, her impossible struggle to balance her life, and the crippling fear of Lucifer destroying all those she loved melted away like fresh snow in the spring sun. It was glorious. She felt Jesus move his thumbs to cover her eyes.

Bright light seared her vision. Jesus whispered a prayer about truly seeing, then slowly pulled away. The storm that for so long ravaged Selah's soul was still, calm, peacefully silenced. She hoped that feeling would last forever.

When she opened her eyes, she could see in the distance behind a beautiful gate of lightening bright bars, the most majestic and beautiful place. A huge palace, in the middle of rolling hills of emerald green. There were trees of every height and color and so many beautiful souls were walking the streets that were paved in gold, scattered with rubies, sapphires, and amethyst. Selah wanted so badly to be there, especially now that her dad waved from the other side of the gate.

"One day you will join him and all of us, but for now, I must send you back. God has given you a great gift, a gift of spiritual sight. You will begin to see things on Earth that others cannot. You will be able to see the true face of evil and cut it down before it has time to act. People who can see like this are known as Seers. You, Selah Jane Moore, are now a Seer, a Defender of God's Kingdom and Protector to those on Earth. You are God's Warrior Daughter."

As he finished speaking, the brightness began to fade. Selah felt burning pain licking at her side and shoulder. She winced. Darkness began to surround her once again, but she heard Jesus's loving whisper. "No matter what comes, I am always with you."

Then the darkness overpowered her, the full weight of her pain flooded her body. She tried again to open her eyes, but she couldn't. She felt a prick in her right arm, though she couldn't see why. Quickly, exhaustion overwhelmed her and she fell into a deep sleep.

Michael and the Archangels had been able to get everyone to safety inside the old church walls. Raphael quickly carried Selah to the back room, filled with cots. It acted as a small infirmary at the moment. She had Jaidyn assist her in getting the medicines she needed. Holy water and anointing oil were needed for the wound on her shoulder. She also grabbed scalpels, needles for stitches, an IV, and all the necessary wound dressings they would need. Raph and Jaidyn began to work diligently on Selah, mending her deep wounds. It was a blessing they had the facilities to do so without having to go to the ER, which would raise all kinds of questions.

Quinn had stabbed Selah near her upper left lung, nicking just the outside muscle of the lower part of her heart. Selah had been unresponsive and without a heartbeat for close to ten minutes. When she finally inhaled with a gasp, they all thanked God. Her heart had been beating rather slowly, but when they poured the holy water and anointing oil on her demon-poisoned wound her heart rate started beating erratically. Raphael knew she was in immense pain, cleaning a poisoned wound burned horribly, no matter her and Jaidyn's healing influence.

Jaidyn immediately began working on stitching the outer layers of skin from the stab wound after Raph pushed more pain medicine into Selah's IV. Selah was unconscious when they finished but finally stable.

Raphael had changed back to her human form rather quickly, due to helping Jaidyn. For the other Angels it seemed to take them a bit longer. However, when Raph came out of the infirmary to report, they each had returned to their human bodies.

"She is stable. We have done what we can, now we pray and wait," Raphael reported.

Tony quickly left to be by Selah's side, while Sean sat on the couch in their pseudo living room, his elbows were resting on his knees. He was turning his hands, palm up, palm down, staring at them incredulously. "She wanted me to kill my sister," he croaked.

Gabriel sat down beside him. "Sean, you didn't do it. You told her no, and didn't act on it. Somehow the hold had been broken."

"Tony told me what she was. He said it would help me, but it doesn't matter, it didn't save Selah." Tears of shame and sadness ran down his cheeks.

Elizabeth was set on the sofa by Michael, unaware of anything that had happened. She finally stirred on the loveseat across from Sean and Gabriel and called out, "Sean...is that you?"

Sean got up to move closer to his mom. Elizabeth must have seen the tears on his face, because she grabbed him up and consoled him. "Where is Selah?" She hadn't taken in her full surroundings yet.

Michael came over to the couch on the other side of Sean and met Elizabeth's eyes over Sean's shaking shoulders. "She is okay, Elizabeth, but she needs rest. She took a bit of a hit tonight."

Sean pulled back and looked at his mom. "It was Quinn, Mom. This is all my fault. I should have never let her into my life." His anger dissolved into tears again.

Michael rested a hand on his back. "Sean, why don't you go with Raphael so she can take a look at you too."

Raphael came over to Sean and put out her hand. He took it gently and got up. Once he stood, she led him to the back room where Selah was sleeping with Tony and Jaidyn by her side.

"Elizabeth, we have much to discuss," Michael stated. She knew him as Dean's partner at the police station. He was sure she had all kinds of questions.

Elizabeth took a deep breath, then tilted her head in confusion and really looked at Michael. "Michael, I have heard your voice many times, but somehow that voice..." Before she could end her sentence, recognition clicked in her mind. He couldn't hide his aura since he'd just changed back to his human form.

"It was you, wasn't it? The one who visited me eighteen years ago?"

SNEAK PEEK OF:

The Fallen

CHAPTER 1

DANIEL

The sweat was dripping down his back as Daniel attempted to undo his restraints. From what he could gather by the damp smell of dirt, he was underground.

Two of Luc's cronies stood stationed near an entryway right outside of the room. He assumed Luc didn't need to bother with doors when his men could act as one. Daniel made subtle movements against the chair he was strapped to, trying to stretch the zip ties around his wrist and ankles.

He hoped and prayed that the others were fine. He remembered a gruesome looking man shooting him in the chest. Blackness, then sirens. Otherwise, the only memories he had of that night were the screams and burning flesh, as Marcus cauterized his wound. "Simple through and through." Marcus had said. "Nothing major nicked."

Daniel couldn't gauge how long he had been in this place. It felt like days, maybe weeks. With no light and continuously dozing off when his body gave up on him, Daniel gave up trying to figure it out.

During the last day or so, someone was coming in and giving him medicine, "to help you heal." The woman said. The medication only drowned out his anxiousness and made him drowsy. However, by the itchiness of his chest, the drug seemed to be working.

Suddenly, the cronies outside stood at attention, and a moment later Luc Vega walked in. The silence was deafening, but the beating of Daniel's heart thrummed so loudly, he swore the others could hear it.

"Well, Well. You are holding up rather nicely." Luc moved in closer to inspect him. "Pity we had to go to such extremes. But you made for an easy target."

Daniel gripped the chair arms as he tried to control his nerves, then turned his head and spat on the floor. "I already told you I won't tell you anything."

"And, I already know who the others are. So...I have my associate here," he motioned to a man dressed in a dirty t-shirt, work khakis, and a butcher's apron. "He will be getting you ready for the next phase of my plan."

The corners of Luc's mouth rose into his wicked maniacal smile. It was a smile of doom, death, and destruction, and it made every cell in Daniel's body recoil.

Acknowledgements

When it comes to acknowledging those who have helped me in this crazy, outrageous, ridiculous dream of mine, there is no shortage of names. But I must start where the gratitude is most deserved, and that would be with God. Because without His constant pushing, nudging, and gentle reminders that this book has a purpose, it would have never been completed. Not to mention giving me second chance at life and to write in the first place.

Next, my husband, my cheerleader, supporter and my major investor--without you and your hard-work, Boobs McGee, I would have gone crazy trying to edit and do all this on my own. You're amazing, and I love you forever!

My actual kids, the constant needling to get the book done so you could read it was what kept me typing. I love you both to pieces, and I hope this book reminds you that no matter what the world may try to do to you, your Mom, will always fight for you.

My Nieces, Nephews, God-kids and the Misfits, this book I wrote with you in mind. Life will give you hell, but God will always turn things around! Let my life be an example of that fact. You are forever etched in my heart.

My family and friends; gosh, if I named each of y'all, this book would have a hundred more pages. Here are a few of you I absolutely must thank:

My Grandmother, Myrtle, I truly love you; there is no other way to say how blessed I am to have had you as my "mother and grandmother." You have always believed in me and my God-given talents. Thank you for everything!

My Sister, Jessie, you were always worth the fight, and you always will be. I love you.

Erica, without you lady I wouldn't have lasted as long as I did in this crazy, cruel world. Thank you for being my forever friend. I will love you forever and a day!

Angie, you inspired me to write and cheered me on along the way. Appreciate you so much for that. I am blessed God brought you into my life in this season, He knew I needed my twin!

Nick, a.k.a. Brain, SillyGirl, and Mickey. You have been my sounding board and a safe place to unleash my stress and fears. One day we will take over the world (for the good of mankind of course).

Kile! My crazy brother-from-another-mother, thank you for being in my life. Seriously, you helped me laugh during one of the hardest seasons of my life, that is a priceless gift.

Maribel, thank you for encouraging my heart through the process, and for your friendship soul-sister.

Zach C., who in all honesty, helped with a significant bulk of my creative process in the very beginning of this project. Thanks, kid!

Thank you to my many mentors and second family, my church family, notably: The Sims, Seiler's and Wise gals. You made my life better by knowing you.

Last, but for real, not least, Erin Liles and Jareb Collins for your help in each aspect of the editing process and helping me prep this book to be the best it could be.

ABOUT THE AUTHOR

DAWN LEE DALEY is a demon-slaying Warrior Queen, who conquers the evils of everyday life with her husband, two crazy kids, and her fur-children, Brandy and Sadie. She loves all things artsy, enjoys ocean waves and colorful sunsets. Dawn also dreams of one day being the lead character in her own books.

.